A STOLEN KISS

"I prefer to discuss how lovely you look tonight."

Isa stiffened, suddenly aware of the heat of Lord Wickton's body and the musky male scent of his skin.

"That can hardly be a stimulating source of conversation."

Barth came to a halt and slowly turned her to face him, his hands lingering on her shoulders.

"On the contrary. I find it . . . inordinately stimulating. I particularly like that shade of blue. You are not hoping to rid yourself of my presence, are you, Isa?"

"Certainly not. I doubt that I shall even notice you are about."

"Is that so?"

"Absolutely."

"Then perhaps I shall take steps to ensure I am noticed."

His hands moved to press firmly into Isa's lower back. She gave a strangled gasp at the intimate contact.

"No man likes to be forgotten, Isa," he warned in husky tones. "It gives him the oddest desire to do this."

Still shaken off guard by the heat of his fingers through her silk gown, Isa was thoroughly unprepared as Barth determi~~~~~
claimed her mouth in a~~~~~

Books by Debbie Raleigh

LORD CARLTON'S COURTSHIP

LORD MUMFORD'S MINX

A BRIDE FOR LORD CHALLMOND

A BRIDE FOR LORD WICKTON

Published by Zebra Books

A BRIDE FOR LORD WICKTON

Debbie Raleigh

ZEBRA BOOKS
Kensington Publishing Corp.
http://www.zebrabooks.com

Prologue

The sneeze, when it came, was violent in nature. Barth Juston, esteemed earl of Wickton, was nearly launched from his magnificent steed by the force.

"Blast," he muttered, pulling out a handkerchief from his fitted jade coat. Who the devil would have suspected that a man could be allergic to olive trees? Or that the evil things would grow in such profusion throughout the Italian countryside?

Still, despite his sneezes, he could not deny he was enjoying his stay in Rome. After the ravages of war, he was in dire need of a measure of peace. It was little wonder he had jumped at the opportunity to join the small guard that had escorted the pope on his return to the Vatican. And why he and his companions, Simon Townsled, earl of Challmond, and Philip Marrow, Lord Brasleigh, had chosen to linger.

What gentleman could fail to appreciate the fierce blue of the sky? Or the grandeur of the Roman ruins? Or the enticement of a lovely Italian serving maid?

A tiny smile curved his lips as the thought of the upcoming evening in the company of Maria floated through his mind. He had discovered his hazel eyes and finely hewed features made him a favorite among the local beauties. It was a discovery he used to full advantage.

And why not? he asked himself, dismissing the renegade flare of unease. The sacrifices and heavy duties that were his lot as earl of Wickton would be awaiting him on his return to England. For now he wanted to forget there was a past or a future and live only for the moment.

War did things like that to a man.

Busy with his inner thoughts as he rode beside Simon and Philip, Barth paid little heed to his surroundings. It was only when a sudden scream pierced the still air that he was jerked into full alert.

He heard Simon mutter something beneath his breath, but he was intent on searching for signs of danger. At last, he spotted what he was searching for. Across the field he could detect a group of ragged men surrounding a crouched figure. It took another long moment to discern that the figure was that of a woman. His heart gave a leap of fury.

"Damn," he cursed as he pointed toward the nearby field to alert his friends.

Another scream pierced the air, and with a brief command Philip plunged his stallion toward the crowd.

Barth did not hesitate. He might be in a foreign land with no true right to interfere in local matters, but he would be damned if he would stand aside and allow a defenseless woman to be hurt by local ruffians.

Sensing Simon at his side, they headed for the mob. Philip gave a signal that they had often used during the war to separate and surround, and with the skill that had been hard-won on the battlefield, they were soon able to negotiate their way through the crowd and place themselves between the woman and the angry men.

Barely waiting for his mount to come to a full halt, Barth was leaping to the ground and rushing toward the woman. Behind him he heard one of his companions shoot into the air, followed by Simon's sharp command.

"Move along. Find your sport elsewhere."

Confident the two could easily intimidate the ragtag farmers, Barth tenderly wiped the stream of blood from the old woman's forehead. His anger only increased at the sight of the woman's patched and tattered clothing. A Gypsy, he acknowledged. He had been in Rome long enough to hear the condemnation and outright hatred for the traveling folk. And among the peasants there was still the long-held belief that Gypsies could be blamed for any disaster or ill luck. It was obvious the locals had decided to take out their frustrations on the poor old woman.

Keeping his eye on the frail woman in his arms, Barth could hear the mumbled curses as the men slowly retreated. They clearly were prepared to offer violence to a lone woman but were far less anxious to take on three armed men with obvious military training. At last, Simon and Philip were standing beside him, and with great care Barth slowly helped the stranger to her feet.

"Are you hurt?" he demanded, hoping the woman could speak at least some English.

"No." Much to Barth's relief, the woman offered them a tentative smile as she brushed the twigs and dirt from her skirt. *"Gràzie."*

"We should get her away from the village," Philip intruded, his gaze still on the retreating men.

Barth gave a sharp nod of his head. "Can you lead us to your home?"

The woman's smile widened. *"Sì.* I lead."

Much to Barth's surprise, the woman agilely turned on her heel and began walking toward the nearby woods. Barth turned to regard his companions for a silent moment. He had no desire to leave this woman on her own. Those farmers would be certain to finish the job if they had the opportunity. Then again, he had seen enough clever traps during the past few years not to tumble into one like the veriest greenhorn. At last, he gave a shrug, and the three men followed behind.

Keeping on sharp alert, they threaded their way through the trees, Philip in the lead and Simon following behind. Barth could smell the distant smoke of an open fire, but it still came as a surprise when they rounded a corner and suddenly came into full view of the campsite.

Barth instinctively held his pistol ready as he watched the old woman being surrounded by a sudden crowd of women and men, all chattering at the top of their lungs. It took just a moment, however, to realize that they were simply reassuring themselves that the woman was not seriously injured.

With a shrug, he lowered his pistol. "I believe this is home."

At his side, Simon gave a nod. "Shall we go?"

"There is little use in remaining." Philip made the decision. "It is getting late, and I have a particularly enticing widow awaiting my attention in Rome."

Barth was well aware of the noblewoman who had made herself blatantly available to his friend. A beauty, although too coldly aloof for his taste.

"Not as enticing as my barmaid, I'll wager," he assured Philip.

On the point of leaving, they were abruptly halted by a young maiden. "Wait. Please. Grandmother wishes to thank you."

Now this was more his taste, Barth decided, openly admiring the dusky beauty with dark eyes and flowing hair. Nothing cold or aloof about her.

"There is no need." Philip spoke for them all.

"Please. Have a seat."

She waved slender hands toward a fallen log, and glancing in the direction of his friends, Barth reluctantly moved to perch on the uncomfortable seat. Soon Philip and Simon had joined him.

Barth could only wonder what was expected of them. Although they had been in Rome for some time, he had had no dealings with the Gypsies. He could only suppose they wished to offer them some type of reward for saving the old woman. He sincerely hoped that it had nothing to do with the peculiar aroma coming from a large cauldron hanging over an open fire.

Before long, the old woman was walking toward

them. Uncertain what to expect, Barth was still surprised when she held out her hands, revealing a perfect rose.

Too polite to protest, Barth watched in amazement as she approached him and brushed the soft bloom against his forehead. At the same moment, she muttered low words that were impossible to decipher. He frowned as she repeated the same to his friends.

Then, stepping back, she smiled.

"What is this?" Philip demanded of the young woman.

"A blessing," she informed them.

Barth was more puzzled than concerned by the strange occurrence. A Gypsy blessing was no doubt as sincere as their fortune-telling.

"What did she say?" he demanded.

The beautiful woman allowed a mysterious smile to curve her lips. "She says,

A love that is true
A heart that is steady
A wounded soul healed
A spirit made ready.
Three women will come
As the seasons will turn
And bring true love to each
Before the summer again burns. . . .

You are very fortunate. Grandmother has blessed you with the gift of true love."

True love? That was her blessing?

Barth gave a startled blink; then, together with Simon and Philip, he allowed his laughter to echo through the campsite.

Barth emptied his glass and leaned back in his leather seat. Although the elegant London gambling house was filled with gentlemen, he had managed to find a quiet corner to enjoy a farewell drink with Philip and Simon. It would be his last before leaving London for Kent. The mere thought was enough to make him shudder.

Simon was lifting his glass with a less than steady hand and glancing at his two friends with a mocking smile. "What shall we drink to?"

Distracted from his unpleasant thoughts, Barth lifted his empty glass in response. "Lovely ladies," he retorted, allowing the image of the delightful Monique to float to mind. She would be waiting for him in the small house across town—a thought that made his heart pound a bit faster.

Philip suddenly joined in. "The more the merrier."

"So much for the Gypsy's blessing," Simon taunted.

"Blessing?" Barth snorted as he recalled the absurd words that oddly refused to be banished from his mind. True love? Not likely. At least not for him. "Curse is more like it."

"Ah, but the heat of summer has not yet come," Philip reminded them in low tones.

Barth was decidedly startled by his friend's words.

Philip was the last man he would have expected to fall for such ridiculous fancies.

"You do not believe in such nonsense?"

"True love? *Fah.*" Philip predictably retorted.

Simon glanced at them both. "I do not know. I loved Fiona this afternoon. Until she threw that vase at my head."

Barth refilled his glass. "Casanova had the right of it. Love is meant to be shared with as many willing beauties as possible."

Without warning, Philip suddenly surged to his feet. "Let us make a wager."

"A wager?" Simon demanded.

"Let us say . . . a thousand pounds and a red rose to be paid the first day of June by the fool who succumbs to the Gypsy's curse."

Barth gave a small flinch. Unlike his companions, he had not been blessed with a bottomless bank account. Indeed, he was already feeling the weight of his most current debts. Which, of course, was why he would soon be on his way to Kent.

"A thousand pounds?" he growled.

Philip turned to regard him with a challenging smile. "Not frightened that you might succumb to the wiles of a mere female, are you, Barth?"

"You forget I am about to be wed," Barth retorted with unknowingly bitter tones. "How can a gentleman find true love when he is shackled to necessity?"

"Simon?"

The handsome young gentleman gave a shrug. "I have no fear."

"Then we shall meet here the first day of June."

Philip expectantly waited for them to rise to their feet. Simon was quickly out of his chair, and after only a moment's hesitation, Barth also rose. With a flourish, they touched their glasses together. "To the Casanova Club. Long may it prosper."

One

The opera dancer was an exquisite sight to behold as she lay upon the rumpled bed. With titian curls, deep black eyes, and lushly feminine curves, she had created a sensation the moment she had fled the chaos of Paris for the security of London. Her success upon the stage had only ensured her position as the most sought-after courtesan among the ton.

It had therefore been a decided surprise when she had ignored the excessively generous offers of protection from several gentlemen for the more modest tokens from Lord Wickton.

Not that she regretted her decision, Monique acknowledged as she gave a luxurious stretch. With her undoubted beauty, she would easily amass a fortune, for now she preferred the pleasure of indulging her own sensuous nature with a gentleman who was not only extraordinarily handsome but a well-versed lover who knew precisely how to please a woman.

Now she studied his tall, well-muscled form as he stood beside the window. A flare of excitement arrowed down her spine at the bare torso and firmly molded legs. Even with his chestnut hair ruffled and his handsome brow furrowed in thought, he was a magnificent beast. It was little wonder every lady in London had tossed their heart at his charming feet.

"Such a fierce scowl, *mon cher?*" she purred softly "What troubles you?"

For a long moment, Lord Wickton continued to stare out the window; then he slowly forced himself to turn to face Monique.

"I fear that tonight will be our last," Barth admitted, not surprised when the French beauty stiffened in shock. What gentleman would willingly walk away from the exquisite temptress? Not that he was willingly doing so, he silently admitted. He wished for nothing more than to remain in London with his mistress and his friends. But growingly persistent bill collectors were a stern reminder that his freedom carried a price he was no longer able to pay.

"You have found another mistress?" Monique pouted, her dark eyes stormy.

"I am leaving for Kent on the morrow."

"Leaving London?" There was a hint of shock in her tone. A creature of comfort, Monique could not comprehend anyone daring the wilds of the English countryside. "But you will soon return?"

Barth smiled with sardonic amusement. "Not without my wife, I fear."

Monique's startled breath hissed between her teeth. "You are to be wed?"

"Yes."

"I have not heard of this. To whom do you marry?"

The image of a pale young girl with adoring amber

eyes and a habit of following him about like a devoted puppy rose to Barth's mind. He shivered. It was not that Isa Lawford was not a worthy, thoroughly eligible young maiden. She was without a doubt all that was good. But the knowledge that he was being sold to the highest bidder to replenish his family's empty coffers made his entire being repel in horror. What gentleman would not detest being forced up the aisle? And somehow it only made it worse to know that Isa was desperately in love with him. Bad enough to be burdened with a wife without the constant concern he was wounding her tender emotions.

"Miss Lawford," he answered in abrupt tones.

Monique gave a toss of her head. "This woman, she is rich and from an oh, so proper family?"

Barth's lips twisted. "She is very rich. As for her family . . ." He gave an expressive wave of his hands. "They desire a title that I just happen to possess. I also possess an estate that is in desperate need of a wealthy countess. We should suit quite well."

"Is she pretty?"

"Pretty enough, I suppose."

"And she adores you?"

Barth gave a sharp laugh. "But of course."

"Monster," Monique chided.

The familiar sensation of being forced toward the gallows rose within Barth, and with a determined motion he walked toward the vast bed. Tonight was his last in London. He intended to enjoy himself.

"I did not come here to speak of my bride. I came here to forget."

Although there was a hint of sadness in the dark eyes, Monique readily held her arms open.

"Then come and forget, *mon cher.*"

Realizing she could delay the inevitable no longer, Isa Lawford reluctantly left the sanctuary of the garden and entered the front drawing room. She gave a faint grimace at the overpowering scent of flowers that were banked about the vast room. At least the bouquets managed to soften the ostentatious formality, she acknowledged. She had never admired the stiff brocade furnishings and heavy gilt molding. She even disliked the cherub-painted ceiling that had been created by an Italian master.

Unlike her mother, she felt no need to hide the fact that her grandfather's wealth came from the shop behind an excess of lavish elegance. Indeed, she was exceptionally proud of her grandfather, who had risen from the son of a farmer to become one of the most powerful merchants in all of England. He was certainly more worthy than her own father, who was the youngest son of a nobleman and could be found night or day in the lowest gaming houses in London.

Not that Isa did not sympathize with her mother's uncomfortable position. Although her vast wealth and husband's connections had ensured her place within the neighborhood, there was a decided air of condescension in her presence. It was little surprise that she insisted upon the largest, grandest manor house in Kent or that she was anxious to secure her daughter in a situation of staunch respectability.

Unfortunately for her, Isa had no intention of fulfilling the latter desire.

Although in her susceptible youth Isa had imagined herself in love with the dashing Lord Wickton, she had long since come to her senses. Only the worst sort of fool would wish to tie herself to a hardened rake, she thought with a flare of disgust. Especially one whose only interest in her was centered upon her excessively large dowry.

No, when she wed, it would be to a kind, sensitive gentleman who would treat her with respect.

A small smile curved her lips as her thoughts naturally turned to one gentleman in particular.

Mr. Peter Effinton was certainly kind and sensitive. He also possessed the astonishing intelligence of a true scholar.

What maiden who possessed her full faculties would not prefer such a gentleman?

"Isa?"

Lost in her thoughts, Isa gave a small jump as she realized that her mother had entered the room and was regarding her with disapproval.

"Yes, Mother?"

The large woman with faded blond hair and pale eyes gave a click of her tongue.

"You annoying child." Mrs. Lawford swept a glance over Isa's tumbled blond curls and well-worn gown of light green muslin. "Where have you been?"

Isa shrugged. "In the garden."

"Do you have any notion of the time?"

"I presume that it is close to lunch."

The air of disapproval only deepened. "Do not attempt to pretend you have forgotten that Lord Wickton is due to arrive today."

The delicate features that Isa had inherited from her father, as well as her small frame and large amber eyes, grimaced in distaste.

"How could I possibly forget?"

"And just look at you," Mrs. Lawford continued in stern tones. "You must go upstairs and change. I will simply have to make your apologies to Lord Wickton."

The small countenance settled in lines of mulish determination.

"I have no intention of changing, and certainly no one is going to apologize to Lord Wickton."

The pale eyes widened. "What has gotten into you, Isa?"

"Really, Mother." Isa heaved an exasperated sigh. Although she loved her elder relative, Louise Lawford could be extraordinarily blind when she chose. "What do you expect? I have been cast aside and ignored for the past five years. Now that the notorious Lord Wickton has graciously lowered himself to pay a visit, I am not going to flutter about like a susceptible schoolgirl. If he wishes a toadeater who will bow and scrape for a morsel of his attention, he should have remained in London."

Mrs. Lawford lifted a hand to her bosom in shock. "May I remind you that Lord Wickton is soon to be your husband?"

"Lord Wickton has not asked, nor have I consented to be his wife," she retorted in cold tones.

Although a doting mother who was often prone to giving sway before her strong-willed daughter, Mrs. Lawford was determined upon one point. She would do whatever necessary to see Isa as countess of Wickton.

"Perhaps there has been no formal announcement, but the marriage has been expected for years."

Isa lifted her golden brows. "I do not recall being consulted on this decision."

"You have always been well aware of our desire for you to wed Lord Wickton." Mrs. Lawford stepped toward her unruly daughter. "And until the past few months you have been quite satisfied with the arrangement. Indeed, you were most anxious to become Lady Wickton."

Isa felt a hint of embarrassment at her absurd calf love.

"That was because I was a gullible fool who allowed myself to be blinded by a handsome countenance and the practiced charms of a rogue."

"Isa," Mrs. Lawford protested.

"What? Am I to pretend that I do not hear the constant whispers of Lord Wickton's exploits?" The amber eyes flashed. "I would have to be blind and deaf not to know he has seduced half the ladies in London. Or that his current mistress is considered the most beautiful courtesan in all of England."

A flush of color darkened Mrs. Lawford's regrettably long face.

"My dear, a lady does not discuss such things."

Isa frowned with impatience. Although she had no wish to disappoint her mother, she also had no desire to follow in her footsteps. Isa's father had remained in Kent long enough to produce Isa before he was rushing back to London and his unsavory companions. He made little attempt to disguise his numerous affairs or the fact that he possessed a thorough disinterest in his wife and child.

"Perhaps they should."

Realizing that open battle was achieving little success, Mrs. Lawford forced a stiff smile to her lips.

"You are simply distraught," she attempted to soothe. "It has been too long since you have seen Lord Wickton. Once you have been together, those silly fancies will soon be put to rest."

The familiar argument did little to appease Isa. "These are not foolish fancies, Mother. I desire more from my husband than neglect and being the subject of scandalmongers."

The heavily jeweled hands waved in an anxious motion. "You are too young to know what you wish. Becoming Lady Wickton is an honor any maiden would envy."

Isa did not doubt that for a moment. Lord Wickton was precisely the type of man to stir a susceptible maiden's heart. And even the hardened sophisticates of London had proved they were no more immune to his devilish charm. His notorious reputation was proof of that. But Isa had discovered there were far more worthy qualities than charm to admire in a gentleman.

"Then Lord Wickton should have no difficulties

in discovering another gullible ninny to fill the position."

The smile abruptly fled at Isa's sharp tone. "It is all that . . . interloper's fault," Mrs. Lawford accused. "Until he arrived, you were perfectly content to marry Lord Wickton."

Isa battled the urge to blush. "If you are referring to Mr. Effinton, then I will admit that he revealed how a true gentleman should behave."

"Fah," Mrs. Lawford said angrily. "He is a tedious bore with no thought to anything beyond his musty books."

Isa stiffened at the insult to her beloved. Peter was worth a dozen Lord Wicktons.

"Mr. Effinton is an intelligent, kind, thoroughly dependable gentleman."

Mrs. Lawford gave a faint snort. "He is the youngest son of a mere vicar."

"What do I care?" Isa gave a toss of her head. "He is the most delightful gentleman I have ever encountered."

At her wits' end, Mrs. Lawford raised her vinaigrette to her nose.

"You are behaving like a spoiled child, Isa," she complained in aggrieved tones. "You are marrying Lord Wickton, and that is the end of the matter."

"Never." Isa crossed her arms in a manner that made her mother's anxious heart sink a notch lower. "I would rather be locked in a dungeon than wed to Lord Wickton."

Her defiant words rang through the air; then, with the timing of a well-written farce, the door was abruptly thrust open, revealing a uniformed butler and an absurdly handsome gentleman.

"Lord Wickton," Rushton announced.

Attired in a dark gold coat and buff breeches, he was precisely the image of a gentleman of nobility— proudly carved features, glossy chestnut hair, and broad frame. Only the hazel eyes revealed the boyish humor within.

An awkward silence fell as Mrs. Lawford blushed, and even Isa shifted uneasily at the knowledge that Lord Wickton was bound to have overheard her impetuous declaration.

There was nothing, however, to be detected on the handsome male features, and with an effort, Mrs. Lawford moved forward to greet her guest.

"My lord," she breathed. "Welcome."

"Mrs. Lawford." Lord Wickton offered a graceful leg before turning to Isa with a quirk of a chestnut brow. "Isa."

Absurdly, Isa felt a tiny shiver. She had not forgotten how sinfully handsome this gentleman was, but somehow she did not recall the sheer power of his presence. The entire room seemed suddenly filled with a tingling heat that pressed against her tense body.

"My lord," she muttered.

"Am I early?"

"Not at all." Mrs. Lawford gave a forced laugh. "How handsome you look, sir. I presume your coat came from Weston?"

Lord Wickton's gaze never wavered from Isa's pale countenance. "Yes."

"I thought so. Quality always shows. I shall insist on Isa traveling to London when it comes time to chose her trousseau." Mrs. Lawford determinedly ignored her daughter's angry glare. "Perhaps, my lord, you will suggest the most talented mantua maker?"

The hazel gaze narrowed. "I should be happy to, if Isa wishes."

Isa opened her mouth to declare that she had no interest in his undoubted expertise with female clothing or in purchasing a trousseau, but her determined mother gave her no leave to speak.

"Isa should be delighted. She could hope for no better counsel. You possess the most exquisite instinct for fashion."

Lord Wickton's lips twitched. "You are too kind."

"And how is your dear mother?"

"Quite well." Lord Wickton at last turned to regard the persistent Mrs. Lawford. "She sends her regards."

Isa gave a muffled snort. Lady Wickton was an overly proud woman who considered the Wickton family far superior to any other. It was only her desperation for Isa's vast fortune that made her condescend to acknowledge the unfortunately connected Mrs. Lawford. And then only when necessity demanded.

Mrs. Lawford, however, preferred to ignore the various slights and snubs she had endured from Lady Wickton over the years and instead spoke of her as her dearest friend.

"How delighted she must be to have you home

again. The poor dear was quite distraught to have you so far away fighting those ghastly French."

"I cannot conceive of my mother being overly distraught," Lord Wickton said in wry tones. "Not even the danger of her only child in battle could ruffle that Wickton composure."

"Naughty boy." Mrs. Lawford gave a giggle. "Lady Wickton is a most charming lady."

"She begs me to remind you of her invitation to dinner later this week."

"We have thought of little else. Isa absolutely insisted on acquiring a new gown for the occasion."

Isa had endured enough. Despite the sharp unease that had settled in the pit of her stomach at the arrival of Lord Wickton, she was not about to allow her mother to pretend that nothing had altered in the past five years.

"You were the one to insist, Mother," she corrected in firm tones. "I argued that I already possessed several adequate gowns for the occasion."

Those disconcerting eyes returned to her set countenance even as Mrs. Lawford gave a strangled cough.

"Absurd. Isa is simply nervous at meeting with you again, my lord. It has been quite some time since you were in Kent."

Isa frowned in exasperation. "Please do not speak of me as if I am not here, Mother."

Clearly unhinged by her daughter's unruly manner, Mrs. Lawford fluttered to Isa's side.

"I speak no more than the truth, Isa. What young lady would not feel somewhat ill at ease?" Turning toward the suspiciously composed gentleman, the older lady attempted to steer the conversation to less dangerous waters. "How do you find London, my lord?"

There was a long pause, and Isa held her breath as she prepared to be confronted by the answers shimmering in the hazel eyes. Then Lord Wickton was giving an elegant shrug.

"Filled with revelry. There seems to be no end to the celebrations planned throughout the season."

"And I suppose your presence will be much missed?" Mrs. Lawford conjured up a coy smile. "Lady Wickton mentioned that the prince was much put out that you would not be joining his dinner."

Lord Wickton grimaced with surprising humility. Isa would have supposed he would revel in his brief moment of glory.

"I played but a minor role in the war, Mrs. Lawford. There are others far more deserving of such lavish celebrations."

"Nonsense." Mrs. Lawford gave a dismissive wave of her hand. "Every brave soldier is a hero. Isa and I prayed every evening for your safe return."

Lord Wickton cast a deliberate glance over Isa's stiff frame. "Indeed?"

"I prayed for the safe return of every soldier, my lord," she said primly.

"Of course," he drawled.

A dangerous glint entered Isa's eyes, and with a nervous cough, Mrs. Lawford edged toward the door.

"Perhaps I should see what is keeping lunch," she murmured as she slipped from the room.

Isa resisted the urge to shift beneath Lord Wickton's unwavering stare. Although she had anticipated this moment for months, she discovered that her nerves were oddly tense. It did not improve matters to realize that she hadn't the least notion what was going on behind that rather sardonic smile.

Strolling close enough for Isa to smell the scent of his cologne, Lord Wickton regarded her pale features.

"I must say you have changed, Isa."

She drew in a steadying breath, overtly aware they were alone.

"Have I?"

"When I left, you were but a child, and now you are a woman." The gaze briefly skimmed her slender form. "A most beautiful woman."

It was not at all what Isa had been expecting, and she felt her heart give a queer leap.

"Yes, I have grown up." She unconsciously squared her shoulders. "Hardly surprising considering that it has been nearly five years since we met."

Easily detecting the edge in her tone, Lord Wickton tugged at his ear in a manner Isa recalled from childhood.

"Is something the matter, Isa?"

For goodness' sake, did he have no notion of how badly he had behaved? she seethed. Did he think she would be there waiting for his return year upon endless year? Well, if he didn't know, she wasn't about to inform him.

"What do you mean?"

He gave a shrug. "You appear annoyed. Have I done something?"

"What could you possibly have done, my lord?" she mocked. "You haven't even been here."

"Ah." He possessed the audacity to smile. "You are angry that I did not write while I was gone. It was reprehensible of me, but to be honest, I am a shockingly dull correspondent. I would have bored you beyond bearing within a few lines."

Her temper flared at his condescending tone. She had hoped to keep the encounter as composed as possible. After all, they were now mature adults who could discuss their uncomfortable situation in a reasonable manner. But a prickly antagonism raced through her blood at his casual disregard for her finer feelings. He was not remotely sorry he had abandoned her for five years.

"I did not care a whit whether you corresponded or not," she gritted.

A brow arched. "Then you feel I should have visited more often?"

"You misunderstand, my lord. I am not annoyed with you."

"No?"

"No." Tilting her chin, Isa met his gaze squarely. "I fear I am simply and utterly indifferent to you."

Two

No one regarding Lord Wickton would have realized that he was anything but mildly curious at the bald statement that had just been tossed in his face. In truth, the young gentleman had been hard-pressed to maintain his composure since overhearing Isa's shrill claim that she preferred the dungeon to becoming his wife.

What the devil was wrong with the chit?

He was the one being forced into this marriage. It was his freedom that was to be sacrificed so she could claim the title of countess. And it was his existence that would be altered beyond all recognition with a wife and family. Anyone would think she was the one making the sacrifices.

Besides which, what had happened to the sweet, utterly biddable creature he had left? In her place was an iron-willed chit with a sharp tongue and unpleasant manner of regarding him as if he belonged in the stables. Hardly qualities a gentleman desired in his intended.

Not that he disapproved of all the changes, he reluctantly acknowledged. Who would have suspected the pale child would bloom into such a lovely maiden? One who would stir the blood of any gentleman.

With an effort, he reined in his unruly thoughts. He had been decidedly thrown off guard by Isa's strange manner and was far from certain how he wished to respond.

"Well, well." He withdrew an enamel box to measure a delicate amount of snuff. "I must say that this is rather a surprise."

She regarded him for a long moment, as if surprised by his bland tone.

"I do not comprehend why," she at last said stiffly. "It has been years since we last spoke. We are strangers to one another."

"Hardly strangers," he drawled, puzzled by her sharp references to their time apart. Had she expected him to wait about Kent until she grew up? Ridiculous. "As I recall, on my last visit to Cresthaven, I held you in my arms as you pleaded undying love."

A flood of heat added a delicate color to her countenance. "I was a child."

"Your kisses were not those of a child."

"You were also the only gentleman I was acquainted with," she charged in defense. "It is not surprising I would consider myself violently in love with you."

Why, the impudent jade.

"And now you are not so violently in love?"

"No."

"May I be so bold as to ask why your affections are no longer engaged?"

A hint of embarrassment rippled over her features before she turned away to hide her expressive countenance.

"Over the years I realized we have very little in common."

"Hardly a necessary asset in marriage," he pointed out in reasonable tones.

"It is for me," she insisted.

"I see." A surge of suspicion rushed through Barth. There was something more to her change of heart than she was admitting. "This would have nothing to do with your regard for another gentleman, would it?"

His suspicions were immediately confirmed when she stiffened in alarm.

"I hardly think that any of your concern."

Barth battled a flare of fury. She had fallen in love with another.

How dare she!

"Considering that we were intended to wed, I would consider it very much my business," he retorted in biting tones.

She slowly turned to face him with a militant expression. "My private feelings are my own."

"So there is another." He narrowed his gaze to dangerous slits. "Who is he?"

"I will not discuss the subject."

With an effort, he maintained his composure. He was a gentleman accustomed to ladies who rushed to please him in all matters. No doubt he was spoiled by his undoubted success among the fairer sex, but he certainly did not expect a maiden to toss him aside for another, especially not one he had agreed to make his wife.

"Do your parents know of this mysterious suitor?"

The amber eyes flashed at his mocking tone. "My father is unconcerned with anything beyond his own pleasures in London."

"And what of your mother?"

"My mother is aware of my feelings."

"And she approves?"

The tiny chin tilted. "Of course not. She desires a connection with your family and is willing to sacrifice me for that dubious honor." She met his glittering gaze squarely. "She, however, cannot force me into marriage."

Force? This maiden had once been eager to become his wife.

"Certainly not." His expression was unreadable.

Clearly unable to determine his reaction to her blunt confession, Isa reluctantly tempered her words.

"I am sorry if I have disappointed you, my lord."

"Are you?"

"Certainly. Although I cannot imagine you are anything but relieved at my decision."

Barth deliberately folded his arms across his wide chest. "And why should you presume any such thing?"

A frown marred her brow. "You cannot wish to marry me."

Barth easily thrust aside the knowledge with which he had devoted years to railing against the arranged marriage. He had at last complied with the inevitable; the least Isa could do was be suitably grateful.

"I must wed eventually."

Absurdly, her features tightened with annoyance. "And it does not matter to whom?"

"On the contrary, I am quite particular," he informed her.

"Fah." She gave an inelegant snort. "A gentleman interested in wedding a lady does not disappear for five years without once attempting to contact her."

Really, the chit had grown into the most unreasonable of creatures, he told himself. There wasn't a single reason for him to feel a stab of guilt.

"Perhaps I wished to give you the time and freedom to mature."

"Really?" Her lips thinned. "I must warn you that I am no longer a gullible fool, my lord. Your practiced charm is no longer sufficient to convince me of your sincerity. The moment you left Kent, you pushed all thoughts of me aside."

There was little use in denying her claim, not when he had indeed neglected to send so much as a missive, so Barth followed Napoleon's strategy and went on the attack instead.

"At least I did not allow my emotions to become entangled with another."

"What emotions?"

His eyes widened at the provocative challenge. "You believe I lack finer feelings?"

"I think you are an incurable rake who devotes himself to his own needs and pleasures."

A thoroughly unexpected urge to prove how a true

rake would respond to such a provocative maiden raced through his body. How would she react if he bent her over his arm and kissed those venomous lips to sweet compliance? Would she murmur with pleasure, as she had years ago? And press her soft body close to his?

Abruptly realizing where his thoughts were straying, Barth stiffened with annoyance. Good lord, he could feel his muscles stirring at the mere thought of holding her in his arms.

"I am disappointed, Isa," he forced himself to chide. "I presumed that you were wise enough to dismiss such common gossip."

Her arms crossed her body in a manner that echoed his own. "Then it is untrue that you are renown for accepting any dare, no matter how shocking or dangerous?" she demanded. "Or that you possess an excessively expensive mistress by the name of Monique?"

The London rattles had certainly been busy, he acknowledged with a flare of unease.

"Those are hardly fit subjects for a delicately reared young lady."

"How convenient for gentlemen that the pursuits they enjoy cannot be curtailed or even acknowledged by a proper lady," she mocked.

"You desire a promise that I shall abandon such pursuits?"

"Not at all. I wish you to be happy with them." She gave a shrug. "I merely prefer a gentleman who possesses no interest in such frivolous entertainments."

Barth gave a sharp laugh. "And you believe one exists?"

"Certainly. There are a rare few gentlemen who prefer to devote their time to improving their minds."

Something in her tone struck a nerve. "Gentlemen such as your mysterious suitor?"

Her eyes abruptly lowered. "I speak in general."

Barth very much desired to meet the gentleman that dared to steal the affections of his intended. He clearly needed a lesson in the dangers of poaching.

"Tell me, Isa, do you intend to marry this gentleman?"

"I have no intention of marrying anyone at the moment," she hedged.

"Meaning that he has not yet asked?"

He watched as she stiffened in annoyance. His thrust had obviously hit home.

"I have said that I would not discuss my private affairs."

"But mine are open to speculation?"

She suddenly lifted her gaze. "Your lack of decorum has made them so."

Barth drew in a sharp breath. The biddable mouse was gone indeed. A fault he would ensure was corrected once they were wed.

At the moment, however, he had to content himself with a mocking smile as Mrs. Lawford scurried back into the room with an anxious expression.

"Here we are, then. Lunch is served."

"Really Barth, if you are determined to wear a hole in a carpet, I wish you would do so in the front parlor." The dowager countess of Wickton, Lady Sarah

Juston, regarded her grandson with dark green eyes. "I never could abide that hideous flower pattern."

Barth came to a halt in the center of his grandmother's private chamber. Unlike the rest of the vast sixteenth-century house, it was comfortably furnished with mahogany furniture and heavy tapestries to soften the block-stone walls.

With a wry smile, he regarded the older woman. Although silver-haired and bent with age, Lady Wickton had been a great beauty in her day. It was said that with her flaming curls and jade eyes she had received offers of marriage from dozens of gentlemen, including a duke and a foreign prince. Instead, she had wed the charming Lord Wickton, who had shared her love for adventure and had escorted her from India to the colonies. Since his death, the dowager had retreated to her private wing and rarely emerged to join the rest of the family.

"Forgive me, Grandmother."

The tiny head tilted to one side. "Why do you not tell me what is amiss?"

Amiss? Bloody awful, more like it, he seethed.

Although it was several hours since his uncomfortable luncheon at Cresthaven Manor, his mood was in no way improved. Indeed, the more he brooded over the injustice of Miss Lawford's betrayal, the angrier he became.

"Isa Lawford," he gritted.

Settled among a pile of cushions, Sarah smiled with obvious fondness.

"Such a charming child."

His aquiline nose flared. "Hardly a child any longer."

"No, I suppose not." A hint of suppressed amusement glittered in her eyes. "Did you not find her well?"

"I found her ill mannered, sharp tongued, and nothing at all like the proper maiden I left."

"Indeed? Well, it has been some time since you have been together."

"So she pointed out with annoying frequency," he retorted.

Expecting his beloved grandmother to be suitably shocked by Isa's unfortunate manner, Barth was caught off guard when the elder woman gave a sudden laugh.

"Did you expect her to be cherishing her youthful affection for you?"

"Why not?" he demanded with a frown. "She claimed to love me. Her heart is clearly of a fickle nature. Hardly a characteristic you would want in a potential wife."

"La." Sarah gave a click of her tongue. "What a boorish hypocrite you are, Barth."

Barth stiffened. "I beg your pardon?"

The green gaze held a knowing glint. "You have been playing fast and loose throughout England and Europe, and yet you expect Isa to remain quietly in Kent pining for your return."

There was no need to make him sound so unreasonable, Barth thought as he shifted uneasily.

"I did not expect her to pine, but I did expect her to remain loyal," he accused in defensive tones.

"Ah." The smile widened. "So that is what has you so discomposed?"

Barth widened his eyes in surprise. "You knew she was in love with another?"

Sarah shrugged, as if the knowledge that her prospective grand-daughter-in-law was in love with another gentleman were a trifling matter.

"I had heard that she was spending a great deal of time at the vicarage."

Barth was beginning to wonder if the entire neighborhood was just a bit looby. The vicar was seventy if he were a day. Not even Isa could prefer a doddering fool to himself.

"Vicarage?"

"Oh, yes, the new vicar possesses a young son," his grandmother readily explained. "Quite a well-spoken young gentleman. And handsome, of course."

Ah . . . a new vicar with a handsome young son. Just what he needed.

"I am glad you approve," he said dryly.

The elder woman was indifferent to his thrust. She was one of the few who refused to be intimidated by his powerful personality.

"Oh, I do. It is high time that Isa had someone her own age to bear her company. It has not been easy for the poor dear to remain isolated in the country while other girls traveled to London to enjoy their season. Every lady needs a flirtation or two during their youth."

Barth gave a shake of his head. He had always known his grandmother was close to Isa, but he did not suspect that she would take her side over her own grandson.

"Do you also approve of the fact that she no longer wishes to wed me?"

Sarah appeared remarkably unsympathetic. "Do you wish to marry, Isa?"

"What an absurd question."

"There is nothing absurd about it." Sarah narrowed her gaze. "Do you wish to marry her?"

He abruptly resumed his pacing. "There is no question as to what I do or do not wish," he pointed out in sharp tones. "Father made a wreck of our finances, and Mother has extravagantly lived on the expectations of the Lawford fortune for years. I shall have to wed her."

His dark features reflected the hint of bitterness that lingered deep in his heart. Although his father had died while he was still in short coats, he had managed to deplete the last of the family fortune on ludicrously unsound investments and vast gambling debts. It was said that he once lost twenty thousand pounds on a single turn of the cards.

As a result, Barth had been raised with the ever-present knowledge that he was expected to save the family from ruin. A knowledge that was never far from his mind.

Sarah gave a vague shrug. "There are other wealthy young ladies."

Barth shuddered in revolt at the mere thought. Bad enough that he must wed. He was not about to tie himself to a stranger.

"I have no intention of searching throughout England for another suitable maiden."

"So, you are angry with Isa because she does not wish to marry a gentleman who is only walking up the aisle to save him the bother of finding another fortune for his impoverished family?"

"Dash it all, Grandmother," he complained at the decidedly unpleasant implication. "What would you have me do?"

She slowly leaned forward. "I would have you seek happiness."

He gave a sharp laugh. Such sentimental nonsense was easy to speak of, but it had nothing to do with reality.

"And what of you and Mother? Would you wish me happy when we are all locked in debtors' prison? A fine lot of enjoyment that would be."

"I doubt that it would come to such drastic measures," his grandmother countered. "I possess a small annuity that would provide a modest establishment for myself and your mother."

Barth laughed again, wondering if his grandmother was becoming a bit daft.

"Mother in a modest establishment?"

Sarah grimaced at the thought of her elegant daughter-in-law. "It would do her little harm to sacrifice once in her self-indulgent life."

"And Graystone?"

"This great monstrosity of a barn would be much improved by a torch and a good deal of kindling."

Barth felt a stab of shock. "Grandmother."

She leaned back into the cushions. "Your mother

has raised you to believe that it is your duty to repair the inadequacies of a century of Wicktons. I am telling you that life is far too short for such grand sacrifices. If you can find happiness, then grasp it with both hands."

Just for a moment Barth allowed himself to consider his grandmother's words.

How would it feel to walk away from his responsibilities and simply enjoy his life?

He could return to London. He could be in the arms of Monique and enjoying the companionship of his friends. Oh, perhaps he would have to tailor his lifestyle to a more modest means, but he would no longer be plagued with the burden of an unwanted wife. Surely that was happiness?

Then a wry smile twisted his lips.

Could he be happy with the knowledge that his mother's pride was forever damaged at being reduced to living on a mere pittance? That Graystone was falling into disrepair? And just to the point, how long would Monique remain with a penniless earl?

No, it was a ridiculous fantasy. His duties were clear.

"A lovely sentiment, Grandmother, but hardly sensible." His lips twisted. "I doubt that I should enjoy living in genteel poverty any more than Mother."

Something flashed deep in the green eyes as Sarah regarded him in a speculative fashion.

"Then what shall you do?"

His expression hardened. "I shall marry Miss Lawford as I have planned for the past twenty years."

"And if she will not have you?"

"She will have me." An unknowing glint of anticipation entered his hazel eyes. For the first time in a very long time, Barth found himself looking forward to the future with a tingle of excitement. Like most gentlemen, there were few things he enjoyed more than a challenge. "Make no mistake on that, Grandmother. Lord Wickton will not be bested by a common cad who does not possess the sense to steer well clear of my intended."

A mysterious expression settled on the dowager's lined countenance.

"I wish you luck."

"Not luck, but skill, my dearest."

"Skill?"

Coming to a halt in the center of the room, Barth allowed himself to conjure up the delicate features and wide amber eyes of Isa. Surprisingly, the image did not provoke the familiar flare of panic. Instead, he recalled the tempting softness of her lips and the feminine curves visible beneath the muslin gown.

"Winning the affections of a lady is like winning a battle," he murmured. "You must plot a strategy, have the best possible weapons, and know everything there is to know about your opponent."

Sarah gave a wry laugh. "Scoundrel."

Barth offered his grandmother a sudden bow. "Now you must forgive me, Grandmother, I have a great deal to do."

"Where are you off to?"

Barth gave a slow smile. "I have a battle to plan."

Three

If Isa had hoped that a night's sleep would soothe her stormy emotions, she was sadly disappointed. For one thing, she had spent precious little of the long night actually sleeping. Instead, she brooded over the uncomfortable encounter with Lord Wickton.

What had gone wrong?

For weeks she had rehearsed precisely how she would inform the gentleman she could not become his wife.

She would be calm, considerate, and firm. She would tell him in concise words that he must find another wealthy young maiden and send him on his way. There would be no need to confess her feelings for Peter or even to reveal her lingering pique at his shabby behavior.

But nothing had worked out as it ought to have.

First, she had been absurdly ill at ease in his presence. How did one pretend indifference before such a disturbingly powerful male? His every glance or lift of his brow had made her feel as awkward as a schoolgirl. And as for the mocking gaze—well, it had rubbed against her nerves in a manner impossible to ignore. Was it any wonder her composure had crumbled and she had come to appear as a petulant child? She had even allowed him to guess her attachment to Peter. A mistake she was certain to regret.

But perhaps worst of all was the knowledge that while she had been goaded into revealing her inner emotions, Lord Wickton had kept his own very much a secret.

She still had no notion if he was angry or relieved at her refusal to wed him. Or even if he had accepted her decision.

All she knew for certain was that he had discomposed her in a fashion she found distinctly unnerving.

In the hopes of clearing her troubled thoughts, Isa had dressed in a warm wool gown of amaranthus with a delightful matching bonnet. Then, with a determined stride, she had headed toward the vast parkland and distant cliffs. There was no better means of easing her nerves than a pleasant walk. And of course there was always the hope that Peter would be taking his morning stroll. His soothing presence would surely take her mind off the disturbing Lord Wickton.

Skirting the lake and faux Roman ruins her mother had commissioned, along with a large hedge maze, Isa followed the narrow path that was lined with towering oaks. For long moments there was nothing to break the silence but the occasional cry of a bird and a distant echo of water against the rocky shore.

Then, just ahead, she heard the sound of approaching footsteps. A smile curved her mouth as she hurried forward.

At last, Peter.

Smoothing her skirt in an unconscious motion, Isa rounded the sweeping curve, only to come to an abrupt halt when she saw the gentleman walking in the center of the path.

Botheration.

The large muscular frame and sinfully handsome features certainly did not belong to Peter. And the youngest son of a vicar could never afford the fitted Cossack green coat or gleaming Hussar boots.

But what the devil was Lord Wickton doing roaming the countryside at this hour of the morning? Did rogues not lay abed until well into the afternoon?

Tilting her head, Isa regarded the unexpected intruder with a queer leap of her heart.

"My lord."

The sunlight slanted through the trees and shimmered in his chestnut locks.

"Good morning, Isa."

"What are you doing here?"

"I came to visit you."

Her eyes widened in surprise. "Why?"

A sudden smile curved his mouth at her abrupt manner. It was a smile that sent a shiver of alarm down Isa's spine.

"Just because we are not to wed does not mean that we can no longer be friends, does it?" he retorted in persuasive tones.

Isa blinked, absurdly aware of just what a magnificent beast this gentleman was. It was hardly surprising that she had once fancied herself irrevocably in love with him, she acknowledged. What young maiden could resist such a male?

Then the realization of the direction of her thoughts made her stiffen in annoyance. She was no longer an impressionable cabbagehead to have her head turned by a handsome countenance and devilish charm.

"I did not realize we had ever been friends," she charged.

"Ridiculous." He stepped close enough for her to catch the scent of soap and warm skin. "When we were young, we spent hours together fishing and exploring the old caves."

"You mean that I used to follow behind you and you endured my companionship as long as I was willing to carry and fetch for you and the other boys."

A glint of amusement entered the hazel eyes.

"How cynical you have become, my dear. I have always cherished my memories of our times together."

A surge of suspicion rushed through Isa. Lord Wickton had considered her nothing more than a pest when they were young. Why pretend they had been the closest of companions?

"*Fah.* You considered me a nuisance and did your best to sneak away when you saw me coming," she said in scathing tones. "You also took great delight in terrifying me with ghost stories that kept me awake at night."

He gave a sudden laugh at her accusation. "You

did your own share of trying to frighten others. I believe poor Oswald actually fainted when you ran through the cave swathed in a sheet and yelling at the top of your voice."

Isa blushed at his words. As the only girl among the neighborhood children, she had often felt insulted when the boys retreated to their secret cave among the high cliffs. In an effort to prove she was as daring and capable as any of the boys, she had crept into the cave during the midst of their midnight storytelling. Then, just as Lord Wickton had been entertaining the other boys with the gruesome tale of the bloody pirate who supposedly roamed the caves at night, she had dashed through the cave screaming like a banshee. She had to admit that it had created quite a stir.

"It was a childish prank."

"It was also vastly amusing," he insisted. "I quite admired your courage in creeping out of your house and through the night to perform your stirring rendition of the 'Ghost of Pirate Cave.' "

She could not wholly suppress the renegade twinge of amusement.

"My courage had me confined to the schoolroom for a fortnight."

"Ah, but do you not recall that I would sneak in each day and bring you treats to ease your punishment?"

She determinedly refused to recall the delightful thrill she had felt when the handsome young man would slip through the servants quarters and to her chambers with a variety of surprises. Fresh fruit, her tiny puppy, Gothic novels, and the precious art supplies that her mother had forbidden were duly delivered each afternoon to relieve her boredom. He had seemed like her knight in shining armor at the time. Indeed, it had been almost a disappointment when she had been freed from her punishment and her afternoons alone with Barth came to an end.

"Did you?"

"Of course." He raised his hand and ran a slender finger down her cheek. "I might have teased you, but I always cared for you."

A ridiculous tingle of excitement raced through her body. With an abrupt movement, she stepped from his unnerving touch.

"If you say so."

For no reason she could imagine, a hint of satisfaction settled upon his chiseled features.

"Tell me, Isa, do you still sketch?"

She was caught off guard by his sudden question. "On occasion."

"I still possess the portrait you did of me before leaving Kent."

She couldn't hide her shock. "You kept it?"

"Of course. I had it framed while I was in London, and it hangs in the front drawing room of my town house. I have had several guests inquire if it was drawn by a professional." The hazel gaze warmly stroked over her disbelieving countenance. "I took great pleasure in informing them that the exquisite talent belonged to my intended bride."

"I think that you must be roasting me, my lord," she protested in embarrassment.

"Not in the least. You possess great talent." He tilted his head to one side. "And I do have a name, Isa. You once called me Barth."

What the devil was he up to? she wondered in wary unease.

He was acting as if he were thoroughly indifferent to the fact she that had rejected his offer of marriage. Or that she preferred another. She did not trust this pretense of companionship. Barth Juston, earl of Wickton, was as harmless as one of those snakes in India Lady Sarah spoke of.

"It does not seem proper under the circumstances," she hedged.

"As I said, we are still friends."

"Indeed?"

He studied her suspicious frown. "What?"

Isa shrugged. "I am simply surprised."

"Why?"

She met his gaze squarely. "I thought you would be angry."

"I must admit I was caught off guard and naturally disappointed. But as you pointed out, no one can force you to wed me."

"I will not change my mind," she warned.

His charming smile never faltered. "Certainly not."

"So . . . what will you do?"

His brows lifted in mild bewilderment. "Do?"

Isa was quite certain he was being deliberately obtuse. "Will you wed another?" she demanded bluntly.

"Ah." Comprehension dawned. "Undoubtedly."

"Do you have a lady in mind?"

"Oh, yes, I most certainly have a lady in mind."

"Good," Isa forced herself to retort, although she couldn't deny a stab of annoyance at his ready response. Clearly, one bride was as good as another as long as she possessed the necessary fortune. "I hope you shall be very happy."

"As do I." At the sound of approaching footsteps, he turned to glance down the path. "Ah, I believe our privacy is about to come to an end."

Isa felt her heart lift at the sight of the slender, brown-haired gentleman rambling toward them. As always, Mr. Effinton held a large book in his hand that he read from even as he stumbled over the uneven ground.

Isa stepped forward with a wide smile, all too conscious of Barth's narrowed gaze studying her every expression.

"Good morning, Peter."

Belatedly realizing he was no longer alone, Mr. Effinton raised his head and regarded Isa with distracted brown eyes.

"Oh, Isa. Good morning."

With a deliberate motion, Isa firmly wrapped her arm through Peter's and turned to meet Lord Wickton's gaze with a defiant tilt of her chin.

"Peter, may I introduce Lord Wickton? Lord Wickton, this is Mr. Effinton, our new vicar's son."

Peter performed an awkward bow. "My lord, a pleasure."

Lord Wickton studied Isa's intimate grasp of the young gentleman with a disturbing intensity.

"How do you find Kent, Mr. Effinton?"

"Quite restful, my lord."

His gaze shifted to the large book in Peter's hand. "Are you also a member of the clergy?"

"No."

"Peter is a scholar," Isa informed him in proud tones.

"Indeed?"

"No, no," Peter protested with a faint blush. "A mere admirer of the great philosophers."

"Peter is too modest." Isa conjured up a brilliant smile. "He has written a fascinating essay on William of Ockham and his ordeal during the papal court in 1324."

Lord Wickton's full lips twitched in amusement. "How extraordinary."

Unaware of the tension in the air, Peter leaned forward. "Are you interested in such studies?"

Isa couldn't prevent her sharp laugh. "I fear Lord Wickton prefers to devote his time to less serious pursuits." She deliberately met the glittering hazel gaze. "What are the teachers of philosophy when compared to the lure of lavish balls and the gentleman clubs?"

"Isa, you forget that Lord Wickton has been performing the greatest of duties." Peter smiled in his gentle manner. "He has had little time for leisure or study. I am a great admirer of all our brave soldiers and deeply regret that I was unable to join the battle."

The hazel eyes momentarily narrowed as if Lord Wickton had been caught off guard by the compliment. Then he was suddenly offering them a bow.

"Thank you, Mr. Effinton. Now I fear I must hurry away. Mother is expecting me for lunch."

Although Isa had waited all morning to be with Peter, her gaze followed the tall form of Lord Wickton as he strode down the path. And even as Peter eagerly launched into his latest research of Ockham's flight from Avignon to Munich under the protection of Emperor Louis IV, her renegade thoughts strayed to Lord Wickton's strange behavior.

She would bet her dowry he was plotting something devious. What the devil was it?

Three days later, Isa dressed for dinner with great care. More than once she had considered crying off from the invitation to Graystone Manor. After all, Lady Wickton could not wish to entertain the young maiden who had tossed aside her son. And certainly she had never bothered to hide her sense of superiority over Mrs. Lawford. But the inward suspicion that Lord Wickton might conclude she was avoiding him out of fear made her resist the urge to plead a headache. If he wished to pretend that nothing was amiss, she could do the same.

Attired in a blue silk gown with silver thread embroidered along the hem, she appeared elegantly composed as she arrived at the great house. For once, even her unruly golden curls had been tamed to a smooth knot and held in place by sapphire-studded combs.

Still, she discovered her nerves fluttering as the stiff-faced butler led them down the massive hall to the formal salon. A vast room with Gothic windows and heavy family shields from the past three centuries, it was as rigidly pompous as its mistress, Lady Wickton.

Stepping into the room, Isa unconsciously grimaced as the slender woman with icily perfect features and an exquisite cambric gown floated forward. As always, her expression held a hint of comfortable superiority as she gazed down her long nose. Lady Wickton never bothered to hide the fact that she considered herself and her son well above the ordinary, and those foolish enough to presume that her air of fragility indicated a weak nature were soon taught she possessed a tongue that could wound at a hundred paces.

In Lady Wickton's mind nothing was important beyond her own grand needs.

Now Isa felt a decided twinge of unease as the woman warmly clasped her hand.

"Isa, my dear. What a charming gown."

"Thank you, Lady Wickton."

"And Mrs. Lawford." Lady Wickton's smile thinned in a patronizing manner. "Welcome."

"Thank you, Lady Wickton," Mrs. Lawford rushed to enthuse. "So kind of you to invite us."

"Of course I wished Isa to dine with us," Lady Wickton insisted. "We have much to discuss."

Isa's eyes widened even as Lord Wickton stepped out of the shadows with a warning frown. She told herself that it was anger that made her heart tremble at the sight of his magnificent form, outlined by the fitted black coat and silver pantaloons. What did she care if he was breathtakingly handsome, with the candlelight dancing off his noble features and glossy chestnut locks? Her only concern was that Lady Wickton was clearly laboring under the mistaken notion that Isa was still going to be her daughter-in-law.

"Mother," Lord Wickton protested in low tones.

Lady Wickton waved a thin hand in a dismissive motion. "I know that you asked me not to mention the wedding, Barth, but really, I do not believe that Isa comprehends the vast amount of details that must be settled before June. We do not have time for such childish fancies."

"I assure you, Lady Wickton, this is no childish fancy," Isa retorted in a firm tone.

A pair of cold brown eyes settled upon her mutinous expression.

"Nonsense. All young maidens endure bouts with their nerves before they wed. It is only natural. Soon you will be happily established at Graystone and will not even recall your absurd doubts."

Isa shivered at the mere thought of living in the gloomy mausoleum, but Mrs. Lawford gave her no opportunity to respond.

"That is precisely what I have attempted to tell her, Lady Wickton."

"You should have been more forceful, Mrs. Lawford," Lady Wickton chastised. "Young ladies nowaday possess entirely too much freedom, in my opinion. When I was young, we accepted that our parents knew what was best for us."

Mrs. Lawford flushed at the criticism. "Yes."

Lady Wickton gave a faint sniff. "Family duty should be taught at a young age."

A flare of anger rushed through Isa at the woman's attack on her mother. Really, she was an arrogant bully, Isa seethed.

"Please do not blame my mother, Lady Wickton. She has been most insistent that I wed your son."

The brown eyes became positively frigid. "Clearly not insistent enough."

"Mother, we shall discuss this subject at a later date. For now I prefer we enjoy our evening."

Isa gave a small blink at the unwavering authority in Lord Wickton's tone. As a rule, he preferred charm to force, but she had to admit that it was quite effective, as Lady Wickton gave a grudging nod of her head.

"Very well."

An uncomfortable silence descended that was at last broken as the stiff-faced butler returned.

"Dinner is served."

Barely acknowledging Isa or her mother, Lady Wickton took her son's arm and led the way to the ponderously grand dining room. Following with sharp reluctance, Isa heaved a sigh. The evening promised to be long indeed.

Her prediction proved correct. After an extended dinner that included soup, poached trout, pheasant, tarts, and a labored conversation about the weather, the women at last retreated to the drawing room. Not surprisingly, Lady Wickton was swift to take advantage of being away from her commanding son to ensure that both Isa and Mrs. Lawford were sternly reminded of the very great honor of being invited to Graystone Manor. At last, using the pretense a curl had come loose, Isa slipped out of the drawing room. One more of Lady Wickton's spiteful remarks directed at her mother and she feared she might launch one of the hideous figures, which inhabited the room, at her head.

One day, she promised herself, she would inform the self-conceited countess precisely what she thought of her and her patronizing airs.

Slipping down the hall, Isa was at the point of sneaking into the garden when the door to the dining room opened, revealing Lord Wickton. Her breath caught at the sight of his tall, elegant frame. It was the first occasion they had been alone all evening, and Isa felt an odd shiver race down her spine.

"My lord."

A smile touched the dark features as he strolled toward her, towering over her tiny frame.

"Barth," he insisted.

She hesitated, then gave a small shrug. It was hardly worth fighting over.

"Very well, Barth."

His gaze lingered on the color in her cheeks and the stormy darkness of her amber eyes.

"Where are you sneaking off to?"

She was not about to admit to such a cowardly act. "I am not sneaking off to anywhere. I merely wished for a few moments alone."

"Ah." A wry smile touched his lips. "I fear I must

apologize for Mother. She has not thoroughly accepted the notion we are not to wed."

"So I had noticed." Isa's tone was dry.

"She will eventually be brought round."

"I do hope so," Isa retorted, even as she realized she was indifferent to Lady Wickton's opinion. That woman would never consider any maiden worthy of acquiring the precious Wickton name. Her only regret was the knowledge that her friendship with Lady Sarah was bound to suffer.

As if sensing her simmering annoyance, Barth tilted his head to one side.

"Would you enjoy a stroll through the garden?"

"With you?"

He gave a chuckle at her impetuous words. "Yes, with me."

"What of our mothers?"

"They can surely keep one another entertained for a few moments."

Although she had no desire to spend more time alone with Barth than absolutely necessary, it was preferable to the veiled malice filling the drawing room. She gave a decisive nod of her head.

"Yes, thank you."

Opening the side door, Barth held out his arm and lead her into the shadowed darkness. Together they moved toward the lanterns set beside the marble fountain. It was Barth who at last broke the silence.

"I suppose I do not need to mention how mild a spring we are enjoying."

Isa couldn't prevent a wry smile. "No, indeed. I

believe we covered the weather quite thoroughly over dinner."

"And, of course, we spent a great deal of time discussing the merits of Mother's chef, although I still contend that my own chef's method of preparing trout is far preferable."

"No doubt."

"So what, then, shall we discuss? The latest rumors of Napoleon in exile? The Corn Laws? The current fashions in London?"

"Whatever you prefer."

Her tone was deliberately light, but at her words he suddenly moved closer to her slender form.

"Very well, then, I prefer to discuss how lovely you look tonight."

Isa stiffened, suddenly aware of the heat of his body and the musky male scent of his skin.

"That can hardly be a stimulating source of conversation."

He came to a halt and slowly turned her to face him, his hands lingering on her shoulders.

"On the contrary. I find it . . . inordinately stimulating. I particularly like that shade of blue."

"My . . . Barth," she breathed.

"Yes?"

It was ridiculously difficult to concentrate with him so close.

"Will you be returning to London?"

A mysterious smile touched his handsome features as his fingers lightly stroked down the bare skin of her arms.

"I daresay in time. For now I am content to remain in Kent."

She sucked in an unsteady breath. "I see."

He chuckled at her bewildered awareness of his touch. "You are not hoping to rid yourself of my presence, are you, Isa?"

"Certainly not." Her brave words were ruined as a tremor shook through her slender body. "I doubt that I shall even notice you are about."

"Is that so?"

"Absolutely."

He stilled as he gazed for a long moment at her upturned face.

"Then perhaps I shall take steps to ensure I am noticed."

"What?"

His hands abruptly moved to press firmly into her lower back. Isa gave a strangled gasp at the intimate contact.

"No man likes to be forgotten, Isa," he warned in husky tones. "Especially not by the woman who cast him aside. It gives him the oddest desire to do this."

Still shaken off guard by the heat of his fingers through her silk gown, Isa was thoroughly unprepared as Barth determinedly lowered his head and claimed her mouth in a possessive kiss.

She froze in shocked outrage as the warm lips pressed to her own; then that horribly familiar thrill of pleasure she had thought long forgotten began to tremble in the pit of her stomach.

It was a thrill that had once occurred whenever

Barth walked into the room or glanced in her direction.

A moan was wrenched from deep in her throat as her mouth instinctively softened in invitation.

No, she told herself in dismay.

It could not be possible.

She could not still desire this man.

Four

Despite being far more experienced than Isa in the art of seduction, Barth discovered himself equally startled by the passionate kiss. Unlike Isa, however, Barth was anything but displeased by the searing delight that raced through his body.

Indeed, three days later, his thoughts still lingered with pleasure over the memory of holding the tiny woman in his arms. He had not expected to feel such a fierce stirring of desire at a mere kiss. After all, he was not a greenhorn who considered himself fortunate after a few fumbled caresses in the darkness of the garden. He had seduced the most beautiful women in the world. A kiss was just another kiss.

But quite to his amazement, he had felt a shock of need clench deep within him at the yielding softness of her lips. And for a wild moment he had battled the urge to lead her even deeper into the garden and further explore her tempting innocence.

A sudden smile curved his chiseled lips. How the devil did he ever presume that his intimate relationship would be more a duty than a pleasure?

Now he eagerly looked forward to the moment he could claim Isa Lawford as his own.

Of course, first he had to convince the stubborn chit that she was destined to become the next countess of Wickton.

His smile dimmed as he recalled the fierce panic that had abruptly attacked Isa and the manner in which she had fled the garden as if he were Lucifer himself. She had clearly convinced herself that he was unworthy of love; it would take more than practiced kisses to convince her otherwise.

But first things first, he sternly reminded himself. Isa would never be lured into marriage as long as she considered herself in love with Peter Effinton. He had to rid himself of the unwelcome distraction before he could begin to use his irresistible charms.

With that thought in mind, Barth went in determined pursuit of his invaluable steward. He intended to learn as much about his enemy as soon as possible.

Not surprisingly, Mr. Portswaite was discovered hunched over a desk in the study. A thin, middle-aged man with a thatch of brown hair, he possessed a shrewd intelligence that had somehow managed to keep the destitute estate limping along. He also possessed a studious manner that would have naturally drawn him toward the highly esteemed Peter Effinton.

Entering the leather-scented room, Barth smiled as the man, attired in a plain coat and breeches, hurried to his feet.

"Good morning, Portswaite."

The steward blinked in surprise, far from accustomed to having his employer deliberately seek out his company.

"My lord."

"How do you go on?"

"Quite well." A sudden glint entered the brown eyes. "Would you care to view the books, my lord?"

"Good God, no."

"Oh."

Barth couldn't help but laugh at the manner in which the thin face crumpled at his instinctive response.

"Yes, a sad disappointment for an earl, eh, Portswaite?" he consoled his servant. "I unfortunately trust you inexplicably and refuse to fribble away the afternoon calculating sums that have already been perfectly calculated."

"Perhaps you prefer to discuss the field rotations?" he asked hopefully.

Barth casually strolled toward the Sheraton desk.

"Actually I prefer to discuss Mr. Effinton."

Not surprisingly, Portswaite blinked in bewilderment. "The vicar?"

"Mr. Peter Effinton," Barth clarified.

"I see," the young man murmured, even though it was obvious that he did not see at all.

"What do you think of the young gentleman?"

"I believe he is a scholar."

"Yes. Is he well liked about the neighborhood?"

Portswaite gave a vague shrug. "Well enough."

"There has been no . . . gossip?"

"No, my lord." Portswaite regarded him with a faint frown. "Is something amiss?"

Barth gave a dismissive wave of his hand, wondering how many throughout the neighborhood were aware of Isa's preference for Peter Effinton.

"I am interested in learning more of Peter Effinton. Surely you have spoken with him?"

"On occasion," Portswaite admitted.

"Does he like to drink?"

The brown eyes widened in shock. "Oh, no."

"Does he gamble?"

"No, sir."

Barth tried a new attack. "Does he have a mistress?"

A hint of color crawled up Portswaite's neck. "Not to my knowledge, my lord."

Good god, was the man a saint? Barth wondered in exasperation.

"Perhaps he does not prefer women?"

The color deepened to a shade of scarlet. "Well, as to that, I do believe he was once engaged to be wed."

Ah, now they were getting somewhere.

"Indeed?"

"Yes, he spoke of a Miss Keaton from Dover whom he was briefly engaged to. I believe there was some objection from the family."

"Miss Keaton," Barth murmured, his thoughts dwelling on a dozen different schemes. "I wonder if he still harbors a tendre for the young lady?"

As if anxious to assure Barth that Mr. Effinton had no peculiar inclinations, Portswaite gave a sharp nod.

"He did speak of her quite affectionately."

"Perhaps I should invite the young maiden to

Kent," he murmured, the vague thoughts beginning to form into a devious plot. "Mother must be acquainted with someone in Dover who could extend the invitation."

A silence descended as Barth inwardly considered the swiftest method of bringing Miss Keaton to Graystone Manor. Across the desk, Portswaite cleared his throat in a discomfited fashion.

"Are you displeased with Mr. Effinton, my lord?"

A decidedly sardonic smile curved Barth's lips. "Not at all. He seems to be a gentleman above reproach."

"Yes," Portswaite agreed in an uncertain tone.

Realizing that his peculiar behavior was bound to rouse suspicion, Barth gave a faint nod of his head.

"I shall let you return to your books, Portswaite. Later in the week we shall tour the estate and discuss any changes you would like to implement."

As he had hoped, the tempting promise immediately distracted his steward, and the thin face brightened with anticipation.

"Very good, my lord."

Leaving the study, Barth was about to seek his breakfast when he caught a glimpse of a slender maiden with a halo of golden curls crossing the foyer. An unknowing smile lit his countenance as his blood quickened in anticipation.

With an eagerness he would never have believed possible, Barth quickened his step to intercept the unexpected visitor.

"Miss Lawford, good day."

Isa came to an abrupt halt at his appearance, her own expression far from pleased.

"My lord."

"Barth," he reminded as he moved close to her side and studied her rigid features. It was obvious she was still disturbed by their impassioned kiss and wished he were in Jericho. "How very remiss of Gatson. He did not inform me that you had arrived."

"That is because I am here to see your grandmother," she informed him in a lofty tone.

His lips twitched. "A pity."

The amber eyes became positively frosty. "Pray excuse me."

He shifted to block her path. "Surely there is no need to rush away? Why do you not join me in the library?"

"Lady Wickton is expecting me."

"Surely she would not grudge me a few moments of your time?"

She remained indifferent to the persuasive charm of his smile.

"No, thank you, my—Barth."

"You seem upset." He lifted his hand to tug at his ear. "Is something amiss?"

Her lips thinned as she sensed his simmering amusement. "I simply prefer not to keep your grandmother waiting."

"Ah, Isa." He gave a low chuckle. "Why do you not admit that you are angry because I kissed you?"

She reddened but predictably refused to concede the truth. "Absurd."

"You can hardly hold me at fault," he relentlessly

Isa swept past the laughing nobleman with her head high, but inwardly she was quivering with emotions.

If only she were a man, she seethed, she would have planted him a facer. Of course, if she were a man, then she wouldn't be wracked with a combination of anger, embarrassment, and self-loathing.

How could she have made such a cake of herself?

It was ridiculous enough that she had allowed Barth to kiss her. After all, she was a mature woman. She could have repulsed his advances. But to actually have responded . . .

Even three days later, she shuddered at her fervent excitement. It was little wonder that Barth was so vastly amused. She had behaved as if she were once again a susceptible schoolgirl longing to be held in his arms.

It did not even help to acknowledge that she had at last come to her senses and fled the garden. She had allowed him to realize that she was still vulnerable to his practiced seduction. It was a humiliating weakness that had haunted her for the past three days.

Climbing the wide flight of steps, Isa entered Lady Sarah's private wing. A waiting servant pulled open the door to the informal salon, and with an effort, Isa managed a smile as she crossed toward the silver-haired dowager seated on the sofa.

"Isa, darling, how lovely to see you," the older woman exclaimed with a warm smile.

Although as close to Lady Sarah as she was to her own mother, Isa felt a decided constraint as she smoothed the skirt of her pale apricot gown. Not only was she still perturbed by her encounter with the odious Lord Wickton; there was also the knowledge that her relationship with the elder woman was bound to be awkward.

After all, Lady Sarah doted upon her only grandson and could not be pleased to discover that Isa preferred another.

"Lady Wickton."

"Lady Wickton? Goodness." Silver brows arched in surprise. "Have I displeased you?"

"Of course not," Isa denied.

"Then my name is Sarah," she insisted. "Have a seat, my dear. It has been far too long since we were together."

Perching on the edge of a cushioned chair, Isa gave a faint shrug.

"I have been rather occupied."

A knowing smile touched the lined countenance. "Yes, so I have heard."

Blast the local rattles, Isa silently cursed as she shifted uneasily beneath the piercing gaze. She should have suspected that Lady Sarah would be aware of the rumors of her and Mr. Effinton even in her splendid seclusion.

"I suppose you have called me here to convince me that I should marry your grandson."

"Good lord, no," Lady Sarah surprised her by retorting. "I am delighted you have cried off."

"You are?"

"Of course. I have always strongly opposed my daughter-in-law's determination to barter my grandson for her own comfort." Lady Sarah glanced toward the large portrait over the mantel. Isa did not bother to turn her head. She had always found the darkly handsome features of the third earl far too similar to the current earl's for comfort. "Having married for love myself, I would wish the same for Barth."

"Oh."

"You seem surprised."

Isa was more than surprised; she was stunned. And oddly hurt that the dowager appeared so pleased she was not to become a member of the Wickton clan.

"You never mentioned your objection to our marriage before," she pointed out in stiff tones.

Lady Sarah gave a tinkling laugh. "It would hardly have been kind when you thought yourself so desperately in love."

A hint of color crawled beneath her cheeks. Desperately in love? Really, she had been a mere child.

"I fear few others are as pleased as you by my refusal to wed Lord Wickton."

"No. Isobella is desperate for a means to pay her outstanding bills, and your own dear mother is quite determined to see you a countess. They will not concede defeat easily."

Isa grimaced. "No."

"They cannot force you to wed," Lady Sarah retorted in firm tones.

"That is what I tell myself."

"And what of Barth?"

Isa caught her breath. "What do you mean?"

"Is he pleased at your decision?"

For no reason at all, the memory of the searing kiss in the garden rose to her mind. She abruptly dropped her gaze to study the clenched fists in her lap.

"I haven't the least notion."

"Has something occurred, Isa?"

Isa paused; then, abruptly, her expression hardened. "I realize that he is your grandson, but he is the most . . . aggravating of gentlemen."

"Oh, I fully agree. He was abominably spoiled as a child, and of course, his undoubted success among the ton has only ensured his arrogance. What has he done?"

"He kissed me," Isa breathed.

Unbelievably, Lady Sarah gave a laugh. "Is that all? I should have been very surprised to learn that he hadn't attempted to kiss you."

The amber gaze abruptly lifted. "He has no right to such intimacies."

"Did he harm you?"

"Of course not."

"And did you enjoy his kiss?"

Isa stiffened. Did Lady Sarah not realize how improper it was for her grandson to be treating her like a common flirt?

"He is very accomplished in the art of seducing a woman."

Far from disapproving, a secretive smile curved the old lady's lips.

"Yes, it is a talent that all the Wickton men inherit."

And a talent they were anxious to share with every available female, Isa thought with a flare of distaste.

"I unfortunately cannot admire such skills," she retorted in disapproving tones.

"No?" The silver head tilted to one side. "How very odd. I must say that I very much appreciated such talent."

Isa refused to blush at the teasing words. "Lord Wickton will no doubt find it an advantage in his search for a new bride."

"No doubt," Lady Sarah agreed in light tones. "And you shall discover a nice gentleman who is very poor at seducing a maiden, and you both shall be quite happy." The door opened, revealing an aged servant with a large tray. "Ah . . . tea."

Five

As was her habit, Isa left the house early to stroll through the sun-drenched grounds. This morning, however, she avoided the public path and instead headed toward the large lake. No doubt Peter would be taking his walk from the vicarage to the distant cliffs, but the fear of encountering Lord Wickton overrode her desire to speak with her dear friend.

Attired in a pale blue gown with an indigo spencer, she crossed the dew-kissed lawn. It was absurd to take such pains to avoid Barth, she acknowledged. He meant nothing to her. But since that unnerving kiss in the garden, she could not deny that she had taken great pains to avoid his presence.

Why did he not return to London?

It was common knowledge that he abhorred the placid country society. And certainly his mother would not desire him underfoot. So what could possibly be keeping him in Kent?

It was a puzzle that she found herself brooding over far too often.

Clicking her tongue in exasperation, Isa wrapped

her arms about her waist. Not so very long ago she had nothing to trouble her mind. Her days were filled with lovely thoughts of Peter and how he would one day return her devotion. There were no tangled emotions that battled in the pit of her stomach. And certainly no traitorous dreams that made her blush even to recall.

Blast Lord Wickton and his troublesome presence.

Reaching the edge of the lake, Isa skirted alongside the glittering water as she attempted to clear her thoughts. It was a beautiful morning. Too beautiful to ruin with thoughts of Lord Wickton.

For nearly half an hour Isa walked through the parkland; then, as her slippers became damp from the grass, she turned to make her way back along the lake. Her mother would no doubt be waiting to review the daily menu or discuss how to purchase the best cuts of beef. She had yet to console herself with the knowledge that Isa was not about to become mistress of Graystone Manor. In fact, Isa had only to hint that she would prefer a modest cottage with Peter for her mother to indulge in a fit of the vapors. She could only hope in time that her mother would accept the fact that it was preferable for Isa to be the happy wife of a scholar than a miserable countess.

The thought brought a wry grin to her face. To her mother's mind, being a countess was far more important than mere happiness. No amount of time could alter that.

Pausing to admire the pair of swans swimming toward the edge of the lake, Isa was startled by the sound of approaching footsteps. Presuming it must be one of the many gardeners, Isa casually turned, only to stiffen in alarm at the sight of the large, impossibly handsome gentleman regarding her with lazy amusement.

"Good morning, Isa."

Botheration! It was little wonder her nerves were on edge. How was she supposed to be at ease when she never knew when Lord Wickton might suddenly appear?

Against her will, her gaze traveled over the decidedly male form encased in a dark gold coat and buff pantaloons. A shiver inched down her spine. He had no right to be so wickedly handsome, she decided with a flare of annoyance.

Even his voice was attractive—a low, faintly husky rasp with a hint of ready humor.

"Hello, Barth." She forced herself to retort in cool tones.

"A lovely day."

"Yes."

"I'm glad to meet with you."

"Oh?"

He moved close enough for her to smell the clean scent of his male skin.

"Grandmother said that the two of you enjoyed a very nice visit."

She rigidly refused to move away from his towering form. She would not betray just how disturbing she found his nearness.

"Yes, we did."

"You were always a favorite of hers."

"Lady Wickton is very kind."

"Kind?" Barth gave a sudden laugh. "She is a cunning old fox who plays a deep game. And I should be very much surprised if she were not plotting some devious scheme as we speak."

"Barth," she instinctively protested.

The hazel eyes smoldered with an inner amusement.

"Just because I adore her does not mean that I am not well aware of her faults."

"Well, she labeled you a spoiled, arrogant libertine."

His head tilted as he considered her words. "I will accept the spoiled and arrogant accusation," he conceded with a lamentable lack of apology. "Did the two of you spend the entire afternoon disparaging my beastly character?"

"Not at all," she hurriedly denied. "We had far more interesting matters to discuss."

A portion of his amusement faded. "Matters such as Mr. Effinton?"

Although an honorable young maiden, Isa was not above lying when it suited her purpose.

"Yes. Your grandmother quite admires Peter."

"Who would not?" he mocked. "He is all that is worthy."

Her lips thinned. "Was there something that you needed?"

The handsome features abruptly smoothed. "But of course. I have brought you a gift."

"A gift?"

"Yes, I purchased it for you while I was in Italy."

Caught off guard, she gave a shake of her head. "I could not accept a gift."

"Of course you can."

"Please, Barth . . ."

"It was meant for you, Isa." He overrode her objections, holding out a hand to reveal a small figurine carefully carved in jade. Her eyes widened with pleasure at the delicate woman with her swirling gown and sweetly smiling countenance. It was not at all what she had expected, and she found herself numbly allowing him to press the object into her hand without demur. "I want you to have it."

"Oh."

"Do you like it?"

"How could I not?" She slowly lifted her gaze. "It is exquisite."

"I once watched you running through the meadow with your hair flowing and your laughter echoing in the breeze. It was a lovely sight. This figurine reminded me of that moment."

She felt that odd shiver once more trace the line of her spine as the hazel gaze probed deeply into her wide eyes.

"I do not know what to say."

"Say thank you, Barth."

"Thank you, Barth," she whispered.

A slender hand rose to brush a stray curl from her cheek. "There, that was not so fearfully difficult, eh, Isa?"

She struggled to ignore the flutters of excitement deep in her stomach. "Why are you doing this?"

"What?" His expression was far too innocent to be

believable. "I have already explained that I purchased the figurine while I still believed us to be betrothed."

"I meant, why are you being so kind?"

He lifted his brows. "Does it surprise you to know I can be kind when I choose?"

"Frankly, yes."

The lingering fingers moved to brush the stubborn jut of her jaw.

"What a sad opinion you have of me, Isa. It was not always so."

The amber eyes unknowingly darkened. "You have given me little reason to consider you kind over the past five years."

For a ridiculous moment she thought he might have flinched.

"There was no hurt intended, I assure you."

Isa took a sudden step from his unnerving touch. She would not be swayed by his charming gifts or his pretense of sincerity. She had grown far too wise in the past five years for such humbug.

"It is in the past."

"Isa, just because I did not shower you with devoted missives did not indicate you were not in my thoughts."

The unexpected flare of pain made her as angry with herself as with Barth. It was absurd. She had realized that he was not the man she had once dreamed him to be long ago.

"Indeed?"

"Of course."

"And tell me, my lord, when did I enter your

thoughts more often? When you were at the faro table or when you were entertaining the lovely Monique?"

A surge of startled annoyance rippled over the handsome features before he tilted back his head to give a sharp laugh.

"Egad, what a shrewish tongue you have acquired, my dear. I begin to wonder if I should feel a measure of pity for Mr. Effinton." His gaze stroked over her delicate features. "Or do you take care to present him with the same sweet compliance you once offered me?"

She gave a toss of her head. "It is quite easy to be sweet as well as compliant when near Mr. Effinton."

"Of course. Such an exceptional gentleman."

"Yes, he is."

"A gentleman without fault."

"No gentleman or lady is without fault," she countered, unknowingly stroking the graceful lines of the figurine. "Some are just more difficult to accept than others."

"As you say." Lord Wickton offered a sardonic bow. "Enjoy the figurine, my dear."

Turning on his heel, Lord Wickton strolled across the parkland toward the magnificent stallion being held by a patient groom. Isa watched his retreat before angrily marching toward Cresthaven.

A pox upon the vexing man, she silently cursed.

She did not ask him to intrude upon her privacy or to bring her expensive gifts from Italy. She only wished for him to graciously accept her feelings for Peter and walk away with the proper dignity.

Surely it was not so much to request.

Entering the large garden, Isa discovered her mother awaiting her with an expectant expression. Her heart sank even lower as she realized that Mrs. Lawford had spotted the tall gentleman as he rode back down the narrow path to Graystone.

"Was that not Lord Wickton?" she inquired in coy tones.

"Yes."

"How very kind of him to call. You are quite fortunate that he has not decided to give us the cut direct."

Isa gave an unknowing grimace. "I wish he would."

Her mother gave an audible gasp. "Isa."

"I do not trust him."

"Whatever do you mean?"

She was uncertain what she did mean. She only knew that she could not dismiss the vague suspicion that smoldered deep in her heart.

"There is more to his pretense of friendship than he would have me believe."

"Perhaps he is still in hopes of making you his bride."

"Then he is excessively beef-witted."

A worrisome smile touched the older woman's countenance. "We shall see."

"Oh . . ." Isa gave an exasperated shake of her head. "I will be in my chambers. I have developed the most shocking headache."

Unlike Isa, Barth was far from annoyed by the brief encounter. Indeed, he felt decidedly pleased by her reaction to his gift. He had not missed the gentle care she had used to hold the figurine or the glow of pleasure in her amber eyes. And even her sharp anger had revealed that her emotions were far from disengaged.

An unconscious smile touched his lips as he entered the great house and headed toward the private salon. How did he ever imagine that life with Isa would be a tedious affair? Since his return to Kent, she had added a much-needed spice to his days. He discovered himself inventing the flimsiest excuse to seek her company, and even when she was not near, his thoughts turned to her far more often than any other woman of his acquaintance.

A most unexpected pleasure.

Entering the long room with avocado-velvet wall coverings and walnut furnishings, Barth discovered his mother seated next to the engraved chimneypiece. Attired in a smoke-gray gown, her hair smoothed to a tight knot, she offered an image of icy perfection.

"Hello, Mother."

She took note of his riding attire. "Where have you been?"

"To visit Miss Lawford."

Lady Wickton gave a disapproving sniff. "I hope that you have managed to convince her that she is behaving in a most provoking manner."

"Not as yet."

"It is all most inconvenient."

Barth smiled with wry amusement. "Yes."

"You must do something, Barth."

"Do something?"

The thin face hardened at his light tone. "Just today I received a message from my dressmaker demanding payment on my bill. Have you ever heard of such impertinence?"

"A tradesman wishing payment for their services? Impertinence indeed."

"Do be serious, Barth," his mother snapped. "We are in a very awkward position, and it is all that disobliging Miss Lawford's fault."

Barth flinched at his mother's brittle accusation. How utterly arrogant she had become. Who else would possess the audacity to blame an innocent maiden for their family's numerous sins?

"We can hardly lay the blame at Isa's door," he protested with a grimace. "She did not force you to order a king's ransom in gowns."

"Nor did she force you to acquire a hunting lodge or a season pass to the opera." Lady Wickton parried in frigid tones.

The thrust slid home, and Barth smothered a twinge of self-disgust. Granted he had always considered marriage to Isa as an equal trade of goods. Her fortune for his title. A fair and proper exchange. But there was something decidedly unpleasant in hearing his mother speak in such a fashion.

"True enough." He gave a conceding bow of his head.

"What do you intend to do?"

Barth narrowed his gaze. "First I wish you to tell me which of our innumerable relatives live in Dover."

Not surprisingly, Lady Wickton regarded him with an impending frown.

"Cousin Arlene and that horrid daughter of hers, Harriet. Why?"

"I wish you to invite them to Graystone Manor."

"Have you taken leave of your senses?" his mother demanded in distaste. "I will not have that vulgar, encroaching woman beneath my roof."

Barth vaguely recalled encountering the large, florid-faced Arlene and her unfortunately similar daughter in London. His most poignant memory was their mistaken belief that he would allow them to cling to his coattail and their grating laughter that even now made him shudder in horror. He would as soon invite Napoleon to his home, but unfortunately Boney could not help in his plot to wed Isa. It would have to be Cousin Arlene.

"Not only will you invite her, but you will ensure that she includes a Miss Keaton in her party," he retorted in tones that defied argument. They all had sacrifices to make.

"Who?"

"Miss Keaton. She was once engaged to Mr. Effinton."

Lady Wickton remained vastly unimpressed. "Why should I wish to invite her to Graystone?"

"Clearly, Mr. Effinton once felt a great deal of affection for her. Perhaps with a bit of proximity those feelings will be rekindled."

"Really, Barth, I wish you would explain why I should be remotely concerned with the vicar," his mother complained.

"Because Isa has convinced herself that she is in love with Peter Effinton."

Lady Wickton recoiled with a profound expression of disbelief.

"That is foolish gossip. She could not possibly prefer that common nobody to an earl."

Barth was not surprised that his mother had dismissed the rumors of Isa's attachment to Peter Effinton. In her mind it was inconceivable that any maiden would not seek the highest title her beauty and dowry could capture. Choosing a husband out of the sentimental need for love would be unthinkable.

"I have no doubt that it is nothing more than a passing infatuation," he assured her. "Still, it seems wise to remove any competition from the field. Which is why I desire you to invite Miss Keaton to visit."

There was a long pause as Lady Wickton battled her distaste for acknowledging her unfortunate connection to Cousin Arlene and the even more distasteful fear of tradesmen appearing on her threshold.

She at last conceded defeat with ill grace. "None of this would have been necessary had you married Isa when I demanded."

Barth smiled with wry amusement, well aware that his mother would have married him from the cradle if possible.

"Do not fear, Mother. Isa will wed me in time."

"Let us hope you are correct. You have made our position most precarious."

Six

Although Barth, the distinguished earl of Wickton, had never possessed the occasion to be seated in a room filled with magpies, he was quite certain it would sound remarkably similar to the squawking, chattering, and nerve-wrenching squeals that had filled his front salon for the past few hours.

Who would have suspected that two young maidens could create such a racket?

Even worse, his simple invitation to Cousin Arlene, along with Miss Keaton, had conveniently been stretched to include an elderly aunt, a grim-faced companion, an indispensable nurse, and a horde of ill-trained, ill-mannered servants.

Now he glanced about the room with a shudder of distaste. In a far corner a clutch of elderly women stitched on squares of muslin while discussing the luncheon they had just enjoyed in excruciating detail. Closer to hand, the ferret-faced Miss Keaton and decidedly rounded Harriet sat side by side on a sofa, both desperately vying for his attention. Predictably,

Lady Wickton had managed to retreat to her chambers with a headache.

The guests had arrived only that morning, and already he was wishing them in Hades. Hardly an auspicious beginning to their visit.

Gritting his teeth, Barth reluctantly returned his attention to the shrill voice of Miss Keaton.

"And so, Mr. King said that he would simply die if I would not give him at least two dances at the assembly," she chirped with a thorough lack of modesty. "Do you know what I said?"

Barth swallowed his instinctive retort. Good God, how had Mr. Effinton ever been attracted to the shallow, harebrained chit?

"I could not begin to hazard," he forced himself to reply.

"I said, 'Well, then, die away. I shall not give you more than one country dance.' Is that not vastly amusing?"

"Vastly."

Thoroughly oblivious to the irony in his tone, she batted sparse lashes that framed a pair of insipid blue eyes.

"Not that most young ladies would not be excessively delighted to offer Mr. King two dances. He is quite an eligible *parti.*"

"I find him a coxcomb," Harriet pronounced in spiteful tones.

Miss Keaton turned to glare at the round, freckled countenance of her companion. Barth had already determined that the two maidens were more rivals than friends within the limited Dover society.

"Only because he refuses to pay you the least attention," Miss Keaton countered.

"Fah. Mama says that he possesses more hair than sense and is on the search for a fortune, which means he can hardly be interested in you, Clorinda."

Miss Keaton reddened in an unbecoming manner. "You are simply jealous."

"Of what?" They had both momentarily forgotten Barth in an effort to best one another. Harriet gave a loud snort. "You have been out for three seasons with only one proposal. I have declined four separate suitors."

Clorinda let loose one of her piercing laughs. "If by suitors you are referring to Georgie and his companions, I am pleased to acknowledge that I have always discouraged the advances of cits. Position is so important to a lady, do you not agree, my lord?"

The thought of one maiden in particular who was indifferent to position rose to his mind. He could only wish Isa Lawford shared her sentiments. That way he could have the lot of them tossed out of Graystone.

"To some," he murmured.

"Pooh." Harriet waved a pudgy hand. "What is position to a maiden in danger of becoming an antidote?"

"An antidote?" The flush darkened to a dangerous shade of crimson.

"Yes, indeed."

"At least my callers do not smell of the shop," Miss Keaton gritted.

"What callers?"

Barth wondered how the two maidens would react if he were to demand they take their squabble to the nursery, where it belonged. Then, with an effort, he forced himself to take a less desperate approach.

"Perhaps you would care to inspect the gardens?"

Abruptly realizing that their behavior was far from endearing to their highly desirable host, both maidens smoothed their countenances to more properly charming lines.

"Forgive me, Cousin," Harriet simpered. "You cannot wish to hear us prattle on in such a fashion."

Not about to be outdone, Miss Keaton leaned forward. "No, indeed, and I particularly wished to speak with you of Lady Claymore."

"Oh?"

"She is an aunt of mine, you know, and I believe quite a leader of society. I presume you are acquainted with her?"

Egad! Barth shuddered. It was little wonder he disliked the chit. Lady Claymore was an abominable creature who clung to the fringes of society and was renown for her encroaching manner and viscious gossip.

"We have been introduced," he reluctantly admitted.

"I must reveal that she has written to Mother and myself of you, Lord Wickton." She batted her stubby lashes. "She says that you, along with Lord Brasleigh and Lord Challmond, are considered quite the most dashing gentlemen in all of London."

"I fear she exaggerates."

"She also claims that you are wickedly wild."

He stiffened in distaste. Had every soul in England been informed of his private affairs?

"Such rumors should be ignored for the fribble they are."

Miss Keaton made a poor attempt to appear coy. "Then you are not as naughty as they claim?"

"No gentleman could be so naughty."

Both maidens appeared faintly disappointed by his adamant tone.

"At least tell me you have met Byron," Miss Keaton pleaded.

Barth gave a faint smile. "Yes, and Shelley as well."

"And Mr. Brummell?" Harriet chimed in.

"Yes."

"How wonderful to live in London." Miss Keaton sighed in envy. "You cannot conceive how wretchedly dull it is to be always in Dover."

"Even with the eligible Mr. King?" he could not resist inquiring.

The shrill laugh returned. "Sir, what a tease you are."

"Yes." He cleared his throat, wondering how the devil he could possibly endure an entire afternoon with the simpering chits. Then, through the windows, he spotted the familiar golden-haired maiden strolling down the lane with Peter Effinton. He smothered his instinctive stab of annoyance at the sight of his fiancée arm in arm with another gentleman and instead abruptly rose to his feet. This was the moment he had been waiting for. "I believe I shall take a stroll. Would you care to join me?"

Both women blinked at his sudden announcement, but clearly unwilling to allow the other to gain the upper hand, they both surged to their feet.

"A most delightful notion," Harriet cooed.

"Most delightful," Miss Keaton echoed.

Barth offered an arm to each of his guests, then determinedly marched them toward a narrow door that led to the garden. Once across the terrace, he maintained a steady pace toward the far path.

"What a pretty garden," Miss Keaton said as she was hurried past the Italian marble fountain and Repton-designed beddings.

"Thank you, but I believe you will prefer that wooded patch ahead," he hastily improvised. "It is situated nicely and possesses a fine view of the parkland."

"So far?" Harriet demanded in dismay.

"It is such a fine morning for walking, do you not agree, Miss Keaton?" Barth deliberately inquired.

"Indeed," Miss Keaton predictably gushed. "I am a great walker."

"You?" Harriet squawked in disbelief.

"Yes."

"Fah."

"What do you know of my walking habits?"

"I . . ."

Unable to bear yet another childish squabble, Barth conjured up his most charming smile.

"Tell me, Cousin, did you attend the theater while in London?"

Thankfully, Harriet was anxious to take his bait and with great pleasure dominated the conversation with highly embellished tales of her triumphant season in

London. Her droning voice echoed through the spring-scented air, but Barth paid her no attention as he relentlessly marched the pair up the path and then at last to the dappled shadows of the trees.

It took only a few more moments to round the sharp curve and encounter the startled Miss Lawford and Mr. Effinton. Absurdly, Barth experienced a stab of relief that they appeared to be occupied with nothing more scandalous than discussing Mr. Effinton's latest research.

Perhaps not so absurd, he hastily assured himself. What man would wish to view his prospective bride enjoying the company of another gentleman?

Offering a polite bow, he watched Isa's countenance harden with annoyance before turning to carefully scrutinize Peter's thin features.

"Ah, Mr. Effinton and Miss Lawford. What a delightful surprise. May I introduce my cousin Harriet and Miss Keaton?"

"Peter?" Miss Keaton breathed in shock.

Mr. Effinton blinked in mild bewilderment. "Clorinda?"

Barth managed a credible expression of surprise. "Are you two acquainted?"

"I . . . we were once engaged," Miss Keaton blurted in strained tones.

"Truly? How extraordinary."

"What are you doing here?" Peter inquired.

"Lord Wickton was kind enough to invite me for a visit."

Peter's vague befuddlement only deepened. "I had no notion you were acquainted with Lord Wickton."

Miss Keaton shifted in an awkward manner. "How is your father?"

"He is well, thank you. And your mother?"

"She is well."

Barth could not prevent a rather wry grimace. It was hardly the greeting of unrequited lovers, he acknowledged. The two appeared more embarrassed than overjoyed by their reunion. Still, they had surely cared for one another once upon a time. Perhaps being thrown into each other's company would rekindle those old emotions.

In the meantime, he was in sore need of companionship that did not include fluttering lashes and shrill giggles. With a flare of anticipation, he moved to where Isa stood away from the tiny group.

"How delightful you look this fine day, Isa," he commended, running an appreciative glance over the cambric gown in primrose yellow with a deep shade of green spencer.

She appeared thoroughly unimpressed by his compliment. Instead, she regarded him with a suspicious frown.

"I suppose this is your doing?"

"I beg your pardon?"

The amber eyes glittered with annoyance at his seeming innocence.

"You deliberately invited Miss Keaton to Graystone."

"Me?" He lifted a hand to his heart in a wounded fashion. "Oh, no, it was my mother who extended an invitation to her dear cousin Arlene and Harriet, as well as to Miss Keaton."

She gave a disbelieving shake of her head. "Lady Wickton has never once mentioned her dear cousin and certainly has never desired her companionship."

He shrugged. "We all alter in our thinking as we grow older."

"And you expect me to believe that it is simple coincidence that her invitation also extended to a young lady who was once engaged to Peter?" she demanded.

"But of course." A slow, decidedly wicked smile curved his lips. "Quite a happy coincidence, do you not think?"

Her delicate features hardened. "I think you must consider me a fool."

"Not at all." He allowed his gaze to linger on her upturned countenance. How beautiful she had grown over the past few years, he thought with an odd twinge. The childish features had smoothed to fragile lines that would rival the London Incomparables. And while her form was more slender than lush, it possessed an innate grace that would capture the most exacting gentleman's attention. He had never expected to find her so desirable. Or so elusive. "Tell me, Isa, why would you suspect me of deliberately wishing to invite Mr. Effinton's former fiancée?"

"I presume in the hopes he will realize he is still in love with her."

The hazel eyes shimmered with amusement. "Why, Miss Lawford, you are not concerned that your beloved Peter might still harbor emotions for another woman?"

A flood of color warmed her cheeks. "Certainly not."

"No, I suppose not." He deliberately brushed a casual finger over her heated cheek. "You are far more attractive and possess greater address, not to mention the fact you do not prattle on like the veriest gabster. Still"—he paused as his finger moved to lightly trace her trembling lips—"there is something magical about first love, do you not agree?"

She abruptly stepped from his touch, her expression wary. "What do you want from me?"

What did he want? he suddenly wondered. Certainly he wanted her as his bride. She had been chosen as his countess years ago. And he was beginning to suspect he wanted her innocent passions. Why else would his heart quicken when she was near?

But was there more to his determination to be at her side at every possible moment?

He abruptly thrust the ludicrous thought aside. He had enough troubles without cluttering his mind with foolish fancies.

"Nothing more demanding than your presence at a small gathering tomorrow night," he assured her in smooth tones.

She cast him a sour glance. "Surely you have guests enough."

"Yes, but since I intend to invite the good vicar and his son, I thought perhaps you would also wish to be present." His smile widened. "I would not like you to think that I was attempting to cut you out and leave Peter alone with the temptation of two young and lovely maidens."

Her gaze unwillingly shifted toward Peter and his former love.

"This is absurd."

Sensing her unease, Barth was swift to press his advantage. "But you will come?"

There was a pause before she gave an impatient click of her tongue.

"Very well."

"Good." Wise enough not to give Isa the opportunity to change her mind, Barth gave a swift bow. "We shall meet again tomorrow."

"How excessively dull it must be to be always in the country, Miss Lawford," Miss Keaton cooed with a poisonous smile.

Isa shrugged with cool indifference. She had endured an entire evening of spiteful barbs and condescending setdowns from the two young maidens. Even Cousin Arlene seemed determined to consider her an unwelcome threat. But much to their annoyance, Isa was impervious to their comments. What did she care of their childish display of ill manners?

Of course, she had to admit that she had been furious when Lord Wickton had calmly announced he had invited Peter's former fiancée to Graystone. She did not believe for a moment that it had not been a devious scheme to separate her from Peter. Whether out of pique that she would dare to prefer another or simple determination to get his hands on her dowry, she was uncertain, but she was determined that he would not succeed.

In an uncommonly defiant mood, she had chosen a silk gown in a pale champagne with a Brussels lace overskirt. Her hair was allowed to frame her face in a cascade of golden curls, and about her neck glittered a necklace of square cut amber gems that perfectly matched her eyes. She would not be outdone by the two Dover maidens.

But it had taken only a few moments to realize that her efforts had been unnecessary. Although Miss Keaton was properly polite toward Peter and his father, she made no effort to disguise the fact that her interest was firmly fixed on Lord Wickton.

Isa's annoyance had slowly faded to amusement, even allowing her to ignore the prickly dislike extended toward her as Miss Keaton and Cousin Harriet vied for his attention.

Barth might have invited Miss Keaton to distract Peter, but she was far more interested in the role of countess.

She glanced toward the thin Miss Keaton, who was seated next to the round-faced Harriet.

"Actually, I have never found the country to be dull," she retorted in mild tones.

"But not even a season." Harriet gave a flutter of her fan. "I should simply die. Mama says that a maiden cannot possibly develop the proper sophistication without being introduced to society."

Isa smiled. "I have no desire for sophistication."

Miss Keaton's expression hardened in an ugly manner. "Well, perhaps you are wise to avoid London. After all, the ton is quite select in whom they include in their entertainments, and it can be utterly ruinous to a lady's reputation to be seen as being without invitations."

"A dreadful fate, indeed," Isa agreed, a rather dangerous glint in her eyes. The spiteful chit needed a stern lesson in manners. "Tell me, Miss Keaton, what did you think of Almack's?"

The younger woman flushed at the direct hit. Isa had suspected neither Miss Keaton nor Harriet moved in exalted enough circles to obtain such elusive vouchers.

The younger woman opened her mouth to deliver a cutting retort, only to abruptly sweeten her expression as the gentlemen entered the room.

"Oh, Lord Wickton, you must join us," she called in loud tones. "I was just telling Miss Lawford of London. Can you imagine she has never been farther than Canterbury?"

The chestnut-haired gentleman, attired in a tailored black coat and silver waistcoat, obligingly crossed the room to stand beside the sofa. He glanced toward Isa with a mocking smile.

"Shocking."

Miss Keaton gave a giggle. "Yes, indeed."

Isa met his gaze steadily. "Lord Wickton, on the other hand, has traveled throughout the world and would no doubt be delighted to discuss the wonders of London."

His eyes sparkled at her devious tactics. "Miss Keaton must be weary of my opinions. Perhaps she would prefer to discuss such matters with Mr. Effinton?"

"How could any lady weary of hearing your opinions, my lord?" Isa drawled. "You are such a fascinating and charming gentleman."

"Quite," Miss Keaton chimed in, refusing to be outdone. "In truth, I do not believe I have encountered a more fascinating gentleman."

Barth flashed Isa a wry glance before turning to Miss Keaton.

"I am certain you exaggerate."

"Not at all." Miss Keaton leaned forward. "My aunt claimed you had bewitched every maiden in London."

Isa gave a choked laugh at the surprising heat that crawled beneath his skin.

"It seems that your reputation precedes you, my lord," she mocked.

"Only a fool would believe such nonsense."

"Perhaps we should ask Miss Keaton and your cousin Harriet?" She gave a slow smile as she turned to the simpering young ladies. "Do you believe he bewitches every maiden he encounters?"

The two gushed, proclaiming him the most delightful, elegant, charming gentleman of their acquaintance, while Barth clenched his teeth at their blatant flattery. Using their chatter as a perfect excuse, Isa rose to her feet.

"Please excuse me."

Barth took a step forward. "Where do you go?"

"I am in sudden need of fresh air," she murmured.

"I will join you," he instantly announced.

She raised a deliberate brow. "And leave your bewitched guests? No, sir, I could not be so cruel as to bereft them of your company."

As predicted, there was a chorus of demands that he remain at their side, and with a triumphant smile, she slowly crossed toward the door, pausing to speak with the vicar before moving into the hall. Once certain she was out of sight, she hurried to slip through the narrow door to the terrace.

She had not lied about her need for a few breaths of fresh air, she realized as she crossed toward the narrow path that led through the shadowed garden. As much as she might enjoy the sight of Barth being tormented by two giggling schoolgirls, she had endured enough of their vicious tongues.

At least she had no concern for Peter, she told herself as she aimlessly followed the circular path. He had shown no interest in Miss Keaton beyond a vague politeness. Certainly he harbored no violent tendre. She could only presume that the forward Miss Keaton had somehow badgered him into a proposal, since Peter could be remarkably malleable when confronted with a stronger will. And then, when the thrill of being engaged wore off, Miss Keaton must have realized her life would hardly be the elegant social whirl of her dreams, and she had promptly cried off.

Of course, Isa was obliged to admit that Peter's feelings for her were hardly violent. There were times she was not completely certain he had realized she was a young, eligible maiden. His only passion appeared to be for his studies.

Perhaps it was time that she attempted to attach his interest more firmly, she thought with a tiny frown.

Intent on her thoughts, Isa circled back toward the

terrace. She had just passed the Italian fountain when she caught sight of two forms pressed close together.

In the shadows it was difficult to determine more than the image of two people locked in an intimate embrace; then a sharp, utterly galling stab of pain lanced through her as the gentleman abruptly shoved the female back to reveal the chiseled profile of Lord Wickton.

"Oh!" At her startled exclamation, Barth turned to regard her stiff form. A shrill giggle revealed that his companion was the annoying Miss Keaton.

"Isa," Barth breathed.

Just for a moment Isa remained frozen in surprise; then, realizing that absurd pain was still clutching at her heart, she attempted to smother it with a flare of anger.

Really, the man was beyond the pale, she told herself sternly. It was obvious he would take advantage of any woman as long as he could lure her into his clutches.

"Isa." Barth stepped toward her, a scowl marring his handsome features. "Allow me to explain."

"There is no need, my lord," she gritted, her hands clenched. "You clearly make a habit of seducing unsuspecting females in your garden. I would suggest, however, that in the future you ensure that you are alone. Good night, Lord Wickton. Miss Keaton."

With her head high, she swept across the terrace, impervious to Barth's demands that she halt and Miss Keaton's grating laugh.

Blast Lord Wickton.

She had thought she wished him in London, but that was not nearly far enough away from Kent. She wished him in Hades.

Seven

Dropping her brush, Isa glared at her painting of the nearby lake with a decided frown. The shadows were simply not right, she thought. And the swan appeared more like a sickly duck. It would simply have to be redone.

And it was all Lord Wickton's fault, she told herself fiercely.

If he were not such a libertine as to seduce every maiden within the county, her thoughts would not be in such turmoil, she absurdly reasoned. It was not as if she cared what he did in the darkness of the garden. Of course she did not. But it was utterly galling to realize that every rumor she had heard was all too true. And to have actually witnessed Miss Keaton in his arms . . .

Her expression hardened with distaste.

Perhaps in London such behavior was in fashion, but in Kent a gentleman was expected to behave with a bit of decorum.

She firmly refused to consider the fact that she had thoroughly enjoyed her own kiss in the garden.

Angrily wiping her hands on a cloth, Isa was interrupted when the door to the library was suddenly opened. She turned to regard her butler with an expression of surprise.

"Yes, Rushton?"

"Lord Wickton to see you, miss."

Botheration.

Was it not enough he had kept her awake all night and ruined her morning? Now he was even intruding upon her privacy.

Still, to refuse to see him would smack of cowardice, and she could not possibly allow him to guess how disturbed she had been by his outrageous behavior. He was just arrogant enough to presume she was jealous.

Unconsciously squaring her shoulders, Isa gave a nod toward the waiting servant.

"Please show him in."

"Very good, miss."

"And Rushton, could you please see that tea is served?"

"Of course."

Rushton silently withdrew, and within moments Lord Wickton entered the room attired in a deep brown coat and cream-and-gold-striped waistcoat. Isa felt a sudden pang of regret that she was casually attired in an old muslin gown.

Did he always have to appear so absurdly handsome?

Slowly crossing the carpet, he studied her icy expression with unnerving intensity.

"Good morning, Isa."

"Good morning, Barth," she returned with commendable composure. "I fear Mother is visiting Miss Griffith today."

He halted far too close to her seated form. "I came to speak with you."

"Should you not be entertaining your guests?"

The hazel eyes darkened. "Thankfully, they believe it is fashionable to lay abed for the better part of the day."

She forced herself to calmly fold her hands in her lap.

"How disappointing for you."

"Good God, I was never more relieved of anything in my life," he growled. "I vow if I had suspected that a gaggle of women could create such a racket, I should have locked myself in Bedlam before they arrived."

She remained thoroughly unsympathetic. "They are staying at Graystone at your invitation."

His aquiline nose flared. "An unfortunate circumstance that I intend to rectify as soon as possible."

She drew in a sharp breath. Really, the man was impossible.

"You did not appear quite so anxious to rid yourself of your guests last evening," she reminded him with distaste.

His lips twisted in a rueful grimace at her direct thrust. "That is why I wished to speak with you this morning."

Realizing that she was giving far more away than she had intended, Isa managed what she hoped was an aloof expression.

"It is perfectly unnecessary. What you and Miss Keaton chose to do is none of my concern."

His gaze narrowed as he studied her pale countenance. "Is that why you looked as if you had swallowed an unripe grape when you came upon us?"

Her mouth abruptly thinned. How could he possibly have noted her expression when he was so busily kissing another woman? And more importantly, how dared he imply she was disturbed by what she had witnessed?

"I was merely shocked at your offensive behavior," she informed him in lofty tones. "Even aware of your reputation, I had not suspected that you would seduce a young maiden staying in your care."

His expression abruptly sharpened. "The only maiden I have ever desired to seduce in that garden is you," he informed her in blunt tones.

"Absurd." Isa battled the blush that threatened to betray her cool composure. She would not think of their impassioned kiss. Not while he was near. "You forget, I caught you with Miss Keaton in your arms."

"She was only in my arms because the deceitful wench pretended to stumble and I was forced to halt her fall to the ground."

Isa lifted her golden brows. "And since she was so conveniently close, you thought you might as well kiss her?"

Barth gave a visible shudder. "Gads, I would as soon kiss my favorite hunter. He at least halts his yapping upon demand."

Isa was far from amused. Did he think her a fool?

"Then you were not kissing her?"

The hazel gaze never wavered. "No. As a matter of fact, she was kissing me."

Isa abruptly stiffened. *"Fah."*

"I do not lie, Isa." Without warning, Barth seated himself beside her on the small sofa. Caught off guard, Isa was unable to move before the length of his thigh was intimately pressed to her own. Through the thin muslin of her gown, the heat of his body seared over her skin. "I went to the garden to find you. Unfortunately, Miss Keaton followed and promptly attempted to seduce me."

With an effort, she forced herself to concentrate on his words and not the unnerving closeness of his large male form.

"Of course. How could I have forgotten your irresistible charm?"

His lips thinned. "I believe the charm on this occasion was the lure of my title," he drawled. "The chit is clearly enchanted with the notion of becoming a countess and is a bold enough jade to use any tactics necessary to achieve her desire."

Isa's anger briefly faltered. It was certainly true that Miss Keaton had made her attentions toward Lord Wickton more than obvious. Indeed, she had been embarrassingly forward. Still, she continued to regard Barth with a frown of suspicion.

"And you did not encourage her at all?"

"Encourage her?" Barth gave a sharp, humorless laugh. "That wench needs no encouragement. She is a devilish nuisance."

"She would be attractive to some gentlemen."

"Not to me. She has been a plague since she arrived."

Isa held his gaze for a long moment; then her eyes abruptly narrowed.

"Good," she announced with a hard edge in her tone.

He blinked at her sudden change. "I beg your pardon?"

"I hope that she is a nuisance," Isa retorted, refusing to dwell on the decided pang of relief that had flared through her heart. Had she not already determined she was indifferent to how many maidens he might wish to kiss in the garden? "It would only be justice after you invited her to Kent to create difficulties between Peter and me."

Something flashed deep in the hazel eyes. "Does it not disturb you at all that Mr. Effinton had once chosen such a maiden for himself?"

Isa was not about to admit that she suspected Peter had been bullied into an engagement by a will stronger than his own. Barth was too powerful, too arrogant, to comprehend such weakness. Instead, she gave a small shrug.

"Not at all. I believe it is common for gentlemen of advanced intelligence to choose the most foolish of maidens when they are young." Her chin unconsciously tilted to a determined angle. "Thankfully, they eventually mature and search for a lady who can share their interest."

She sensed more than felt him stiffen. "A lady such as yourself?"

"Perhaps."

A thin, humorless smile twisted his firm lips. "What a waste that would be, my dear."

"Why?" She instinctively bristled at his condemning tone. "Because Peter cannot trace his ancestors back to William the Conqueror?"

"No, because he is a scholar, and like all scholars, he is consumed by his passion for learning. A mere wife would claim but a small token of his attention." The glittering gaze deliberately lowered to the soft fullness of her mouth. "But perhaps you are too prosaic to wish for a husband that would prefer to kiss those tender lips than to pore over musty manuscripts?"

A sharp, wholly unwelcome stab of excitement pierced deep within her.

No.

He would not be allowed to stir such sensations again. They led a perfectly reasonable woman to behave as a witless fool. She had learned her lesson all too well.

"I am prosaic enough to desire a husband who will be faithful and dependable," she informed him in cool tones. "My father is ample proof that a gentleman who prefers kisses is rarely discriminate as to whose lips he is kissing."

He frowned as if caught off guard by her accusation. "You cannot judge all gentlemen by your father, Isa."

"No?" She met his gaze squarely. "I suppose you mean to imply you are different?"

He paused, as if to consider his response. The challenge in her expression warned him she would not be eased with a glib reply.

"I would never deliberately hurt you," he at last replied.

A wry smile twisted her lips. He would never understand. He had already hurt her more than she could bear.

"No, you will not," she agreed in low tones. "I have no intention of giving you the opportunity."

Barth reached out to grasp her hand, his expression grim. "Isa . . ."

His words were interrupted as the door was thrust open, revealing the housekeeper with a large tray. With a flare of relief, Isa surged to her feet.

"Oh, good . . . tea."

Two hours later, Barth paced through his grandmother's private chambers with a distinct sense of annoyance.

Hell's teeth, he silently cursed.

What mere gentleman ever hoped to understand the incomprehensible workings of the female mind?

One moment they were smothering a gentleman with their demanding attentions, and the next they were treating him as if he had crawled from beneath a moldy rock.

It was enough to drive one batty.

Seated on the sofa, the silver-haired dowager watched the distracted pacing with a well-hidden sense of satisfaction. She had never seen her grandson so discomposed. His usual air of lazy amusement was decidedly absent. It was a most encouraging sign.

"I see I shall have to have this carpet replaced before the year is out," she commented with a faint smile.

Barth came to an abrupt halt, a rueful grimace twisting his features.

"I am sorry, Grandmother."

The older woman settled herself more comfortably in the satin cushions.

"I have noted that you have not brought your guests to visit me."

Barth gave a short laugh. "Consider yourself fortunate. Two more doltish maidens I have yet to encounter."

"Then you have not chosen one to be your wife?"

"Good God, no," Barth denied, wondering how anyone could possibly imagine he would consider Miss Keaton or Cousin Harriet as more than an unwelcome nuisance. "I have only suffered the presence of my guests because Miss Keaton was once engaged to Peter Effinton."

Lady Sarah was swift to grasp his devious intent. "Ah, your grand battle plan."

"Precisely."

Lady Sarah's lips seemed to twitch. "And how do you progress?"

Barth regarded his grandmother with a gathering frown of suspicion. If he did not know better, he would have suspected that the old fox found his troubles vastly amusing.

"Devilishly bad, if you must know," he confessed

in a growl. "Not only did Miss Keaton prove to be a most inadequate distraction to Mr. Effinton, but she has behaved like a perfect fool."

"Meaning that she decided she preferred an earl to a mere vicar's son?" Lady Sarah demanded; then, as Barth's eyes widened at her intuitive guess, she gave a tinkling laugh. "Really, Barth, what did you expect?"

"I thought young maidens were supposed to be romantically devoted to their first loves."

Lady Sarah gave a click of her tongue. "From the few glimpses I have observed of Miss Keaton, I would hazard she is far too silly to ever be truly devoted. Her emotions are no doubt as shallow as her thoughts."

"So I have discovered," Barth muttered.

"Besides, you can hardly blame a maiden for wishing to better her position," Lady Sarah continued.

"Egad. The chit actually attempted to seduce me in the garden."

Lady Sarah gave another laugh. "How distressful for you."

"As it happens, Isa was also in the garden," he said in grim tones. His grandmother clearly did not comprehend the severity of the situation. "Miss Keaton's shameless behavior has only furthered Isa's belief that I am a frivolous rake."

"But, my dearest Barth, you are a rake."

Barth was not at all amused. Was it not annoying enough to be constantly compared to Isa's scapegrace father? He was not a hardened gambler, nor did he host vulgar parties in the back of gin houses with common prostitutes. Indeed, his lifestyle was quite mild when compared to many of his associates.

"I am no different than any other gentleman who wishes to enjoy a bit of life before taking on the burdens of a wife and family," he retorted in defensive tones. "Certainly no one is taking Brasleigh or Challmond to task for their behavior."

His grandmother tilted her head to one side. "Brasleigh and Challmond?"

"We served in the same regiment."

Lady Sarah abruptly narrowed her gaze. "I believe I once knew a Lady Brasleigh. A most tedious woman. Always imagining herself to be ill."

Although Philip had not been one to confide his private troubles, Barth had been aware of the rumors surrounding Lady Brasleigh. It was said that the woman was thoroughly self-absorbed and made constant demands upon her son for attention.

"Yes, I believe she has been a decided burden upon Brasleigh."

"These are friends of yours?" Lady Sarah demanded.

A sudden smile eased the tension marring the handsome features. He had never felt as close to anyone as he did to Philip and Simon.

"More like brothers."

"And they are about to wed?"

"Ha." Barth gave a laugh at the mere notion. Both gentlemen were confirmed bachelors and fortunate enough in their positions not to be forced into the parson's mousetrap. Unlike himself. "Napoleon will be crowned king of England before those two would allow themselves to be leg-shackled."

Lady Sarah met his gaze squarely. "So there is no one to be concerned if they chose to be less than circumspect with the fairer sex."

Barth smiled wryly, recalling the unpleasant gossip that had seemed to travel throughout the length and breadth of England. Perhaps selfishly, he had never considered how his numerous affairs would affect Isa. Indeed, it had never occurred to him that she would ever be aware of his life in London at all. Now he could only wish he had been more discreet. He had been honest when he had assured Isa he had no desire to hurt her. He might rail at a fate that forced him to wed, but he was beginning to accept the fact that he could do far worse than have Isa as his bride.

"Point taken, Grandmother," he conceded in dry tones.

"What shall you do?"

Placing his hands behind his back, Barth paced toward the window and stared unseeing at the vast terraced garden and distant parkland.

"First, I shall send Miss Keaton and Cousin Harriet packing with all possible speed."

"Perhaps easier said than done," his grandmother warned. "A determined miss can find any number of excuses to prolong her stay near an eligible bachelor."

Barth's countenance hardened. "If necessary, I shall bundle them into their carriage and drive them to Dover myself."

Clearly realizing that her grandson meant every

word, Lady Sarah turned her attention to the larger problem at hand.

"And then?"

"Then I shall endeavor to find another means of ridding myself of Mr. Effinton."

"Another maiden?"

A frown gathered on Barth's wide brow. "Certainly not. Mr. Effinton is clearly less interested in ladies than in his studies."

"How very disobliging of him."

Barth ignored his grandmother's teasing as a most brilliant notion flashed through his mind. Of course, he silently congratulated himself. He was a fool not to have thought of it sooner.

"Perhaps not," he murmured.

"What do you mean?"

Turning about, Barth met his grandmother's curious gaze. "Mr. Effinton is at best a distracted suitor," he explained. "I believe that he seeks the company of Isa more out of desperation for an intellectual conversation than any overwhelming passion."

A shrewd glint entered the jade eyes. "For now."

Realizing that his grandmother was right and that with time Mr. Effinton would no doubt drift into deeper emotions, Barth became more determined to see his plot through.

"What would occur if he were suddenly surrounded by gentlemen who shared his scholarly interest?"

"I should imagine he would be delighted."

"Delighted enough to become oblivious to Isa," he continued, the fine features set in lines of determination. "Pardon me, Grandmother, I must send my groom to London."

"Barth," Lady Sarah halted her grandson's abrupt exit. "You really are a scoundrel."

Lord Wickton acknowledged the thrust with an elegant bow and his most roguish smile.

"Yes."

Eight

"So you see, his entire philosophy was centered on the simplicity of life."

Abruptly realizing that Peter was regarding her with an expectant expression, Isa hastily recalled her wandering thoughts and suppressed a treacherous yawn. It was not that she did not find Peter's research fascinating, she attempted to reassure herself. Indeed, it was quite gratifying for a gentleman to speak with her of philosophy and politics rather than presume that a mere woman could not comprehend such complicated matters. And certainly she was not so silly as to desire a gentleman who wasted her days with empty compliments and shallow flirtations.

Still, as she sat beside Peter on the sofa in the front parlor, she could not deny a tiny pang of regret. She would not mind if he were a bit more . . . dashing, she had to admit.

Against her will, the image of dark features and gold-flecked hazel eyes rose to mind. What would Barth do if they were alone on this sofa?

Certainly he would not have devoted two hours to

discussing his previous night's readings. No. More than likely he would have pulled her into his arms and made her head spin with his heated kisses.

A thoroughly unwelcome tingle of excitement raced through her body.

Such kisses . . .

"Isa, are you attending me?"

A flare of color rushed to Isa's cheeks as she firmly chastised her wayward thoughts.

She was shameless.

"Yes, of course I am."

Once more confident his audience was giving him the proper attention, Peter continued his lecture.

"It is all so much clearer, since I have a copy of the original manuscript. Too much can be altered in the translation." He held out a large sheet of parchment covered in neat script. "You see the verb here . . ."

"Peter." Isa desperately interrupted the droning voice. She simply could not bear another two hours of such tedious conversation.

"Yes?"

"Could we not perhaps spend the day upon the lake?"

She might as well have suggested that they traverse to the colonies for the shock that widened Peter's eyes.

"The lake?"

"Yes. I could have Cook prepare us a basket, and we could row to the island." She smiled in a pleading fashion, not about to admit that she had already requested that Cook prepare a romantic luncheon and pack it into a wicker basket just in the hopes of luring Peter away from his manuscripts.

Peter grimaced as he glanced toward a window where the sun tumbled happily into the room.

"There is rather a breeze."

"Nonsense," Isa retorted. "It is a lovely day."

Peter hastily changed tactics. "Yes, well, perhaps your mother would not quite care for the scheme."

"What is not to care?" Isa demanded. "We shall be in perfect view of the entire household. There could be nothing improper."

"I do not know." Peter gave a delicate shudder. "I have no particular fondness for water."

Isa bit back a sigh of impatience. Really, she was not asking so very much, was she?

"We shall not be in the water. We shall be upon the island enjoying a lovely picnic." She once again flashed her most persuasive smile. "Do say yes."

Clearly cornered, Peter had little choice but to give a vague flutter of his thin hands.

"I suppose we might."

"Superb." Isa abruptly rose to her feet. "I shall go fetch our food while you see to the boat."

Peter blinked. "Now?"

"But of course. It shall be a delightful change."

"I suppose," Peter muttered, far from convinced. "I shall join you at the lake in a moment."

Unwilling to give Peter any further opportunities to argue, Isa swept from the room and made her way toward the back of the house. Perhaps she was being somewhat devious, she conceded, but she had to do something. Peter would never notice her in a romantic manner unless she took matters into her own hands.

And so, putting aside her vague sense of guilt at the lengths she had gone to, Isa entered the vast kitchen to locate the decidedly plump cook, who was busily kneading a large ball of dough.

"Mrs. Sculder."

Glancing up, the middle-aged servant with a round face and disorderly gray hair regarded Isa with a sudden smile.

"My dear, don't you look lovely."

Isa glanced down at the elegant gown in the shade of bluebells. It was one of her favorites as well as being one of her most flattering.

"Thank you, Mrs. Sculder. Is the basket prepared?"

"Aye." The cook nodded her head toward a long table on which a basket was covered with a white cloth. "Although it be a waste of good food, if you ask me."

Isa gave a sudden blink. "I beg your pardon?"

"I might as well have boiled a turnip for all the notice Mr. Effinton will give my fine pheasant and mushroom pie," Mrs. Sculder mourned, her artistic soul wounded by Peter's philistine disregard for her creations. "Now, Lord Wickton. He is a gentleman who appreciates a well-cooked meal. He is always complimenting me on my way with pastries."

Isa frowned in exasperation. "Lord Wickton possesses a keen appreciation of his own pleasures."

A surprisingly naughty smile curved the older woman's lips.

"A lady could do worse."

"Not you, too, Mrs. Sculder," Isa groaned. For goodness' sake, had Lord Wickton managed to charm every female in the country? She heartily wished never to hear his name spoken again.

"I only desire you to find a gentleman that will appreciate you as you deserve."

"What gentleman ever truly appreciates a lady, Mrs. Sculder?" Isa demanded. "They expect us to provide them comfort, see to their needs, and entertain them when necessary. And, of course, to gracefully fade into the background when we interfere in their privacy, which appears to be the vast majority of the time."

Mrs. Sculder gave a disapproving click of her tongue at Isa's words.

"You are too young for such thoughts."

"You think I should still be a giddy schoolgirl in love with every fribble who might pay her a pretty compliment?" Isa demanded, recalling her once naive passion with a shudder of embarrassment. "No, thank you. I prefer a gentleman who possesses substance, not charm."

"Substance?" Mrs. Sculder kneaded the dough with a bit more enthusiasm than necessary. "More like soggy pudding."

Isa resisted the urge to defend Peter. *Why bother?* Mrs. Sculder was clearly as blinded by Lord Wickton's charm as every other woman.

"I must not keep Mr. Effinton waiting."

Turning about, she moved to gather the large basket and left the kitchen. It was only a short distance to a side door that led to the garden. Stepping into the warm sunshine, Isa felt a measure of her annoyance fading. She would not allow thoughts of Lord Wickton to ruin her day. Not when she was determined to capture Peter's elusive attention. Sternly forcing her thoughts toward the upcoming picnic, Isa made her way through the garden and into the parkland. Before long, she had reached the short dock where Peter was struggling to untie the small rowboat from its post.

"Are we ready?"

Glancing up from his task, Peter cast her a decided frown. "I do not know. That cloud appears particularly ominous."

Isa dutifully scanned the brilliantly blue sky for the treacherous cloud, only to discover a distant puff of white.

"I believe that all will be well," she reassured.

"I suppose," Peter agreed with obvious reluctance. "Here."

Taking the basket, he prepared to help Isa into the boat, but she needed no aid. With practiced grace, she leaped into the center of the boat; then, sitting down, she took the basket and tucked it beneath her seat. Unfortunately, Peter possessed none of her skill, and after finishing untying the rope, he awkwardly stepped down into the boat and immediately set it rocking in an alarming fashion.

"Careful," Isa called as she grasped the sides of the boat.

Peter fell back onto his seat, his weight tipping them to one side.

"Good lord, I wish the blasted thing would hold steady."

"You must sit in the center."

Peter obligingly shifted to the center, then set the boat rocking once again as he reached for the oars.

"I thought carriages were treacherous beasts."

"You must not fidget," she commanded.

"Easy enough to say," Peter muttered as he struggled to push away from the dock and set the oars in motion.

There was a great deal of splashing, and more than once Isa feared they would not even make it away from the shore, but after much struggle, Peter managed to head them toward the small island in the middle of the lake.

"There, is this not pleasant?" Isa encouraged.

Peter grimaced, his face red from the unaccustomed exertion.

"It seems rather foolish to go to such effort when we might have eaten in comfort at your home."

"But is it not nice to be among nature?"

"I prefer a less damp nature," he complained.

"You will enjoy the island."

"If you say."

"There are flowers and birds and a host of butterflies."

"And insects and . . ." His words trailed away as a sudden breeze danced over the lake. Abruptly, he gave an exclamation of disgust. "My hat."

Isa watched the black hat fly off his head and skip over the water. Then, with a sudden flare of disbelief, she realized that Peter was instinctively attempting to retrieve the renegade article.

"No, Peter, wait . . ." she urgently commanded, but it was far too late.

Feeling the boat tipping, Peter lunged in the opposite direction and only succeeded in overturning them with a resounding splash.

Thoroughly at home in the water, Isa swiftly resurfaced despite her clinging skirts. Within moments, Peter also surfaced, but with such coughing and flailing of his arms, it was obvious he was unable to swim.

"Help . . ." He coughed.

Swift to realize the danger, Isa struggled to swim to his aid.

"Peter, you must relax," she urged as she attempted to avoid his swinging arms.

"Help."

Debating whether it would be more prudent to approach from behind, Isa was startled as another head abruptly crested the water directly beside her. The flare of shock was swiftly replaced by that of overwhelming relief at the sight of Barth's grim countenance.

"Thank God," she breathed.

"Lean against me," he ordered.

"No, I can swim. You must help Peter."

The hazel eyes seared over her worried features before turning to regard the young man flailing in desperation.

"For God's sake," he muttered.

"Help," Peter yelped.

"You are sure?" Barth demanded of Isa.

"You taught me yourself."

A sudden smile curved the masculine lips at the memory of summer days spent in the cove and the tenacious young girl who refused to be outdone in anything, including a bracing swim in the chilled water.

"So I did." With a concise motion, Barth swam forward and grasped Peter with one arm about the neck. Isa bit back her instinctive protest as Barth began swimming toward the shore. It was obviously the best method to haul the still-struggling Peter out of the water, even if it did appear less than sympathetic.

Beginning to shiver, Isa followed close behind. All in all, the day had turned out to be a complete disaster. Not only had the romantic picnic she had envisioned been reduced to a soggy mess, but she had nearly managed to kill Peter with her selfish demands.

Battling her clinging skirt, Isa swam to shore. Barth had already laid Peter on the grass, and she moved to stand next to him.

"Shall I go for a servant?" she demanded.

Peter coughed, struggling to his feet. He appeared decidedly miserable in his dripping clothes and his hair matted to his narrow head.

"No," he insisted with another cough. "No, I only wish to go home."

"But you need to dry off."

"Please, Isa, I only wish to go home."

"I will have my carriage take you home." Barth took charge, lifting an arm toward the groom, who had obviously been ordered to remain with the high-perch phaeton and perfectly matched grays.

"Thank you, my lord." With an awkward bow, Peter trudged to the waiting carriage and allowed the groom to help him onto the narrow seat. Isa watched in silence as the groom vaulted beside the shivering Peter and with a brief nod toward Barth set the grays in motion.

"And now for you," Barth announced in firm tones.

"What?" Slowly turning, Isa was caught off guard as Barth stepped forward and swept her off her feet, cradling her against his chest. Her heart slammed against her ribs as she gazed in shock at the suddenly near hazel eyes. Before leaping into the water, he had stripped off his boots and coat, and now Isa could easily feel the heat of his body through his damp lawn shirt. It was a decidedly disturbing sensation. "Barth, put me down."

Already heading toward Cresthaven, Barth smiled into her wide eyes.

"You have had a shock," he retorted.

"Ludicrous," she breathed, shuddering at the feel of his powerful muscles rippling against her delicate form. Unlike Peter, who had appeared worse for his dunking, Barth only seemed more poignantly masculine, with his chestnut hair tousled and his clothes clinging to his strong frame. "It would take more than a mild tumble into perfectly calm water to give me a shock."

The hazel eyes glinted. "Then why are you shivering?"

"Because I am cold," she gritted.

"All the more reason to hurry you inside."

Annoying man.

"We could hurry much faster if only you would put me down."

His long strides never faltered. "And have you stumbling over your wet skirt?"

Botheration. Did he have an answer for everything?

"You are without a doubt the most annoying gentleman I have ever encountered," she informed him.

"I?" His lips twisted in a wry smile. "I did not possess the ill grace to tumble you into the water. Indeed, I was the one attempting to save you. Most ladies would consider me the hero, not the villain, of the piece."

That he was absolutely right did not ease her irritation. Of course he was the hero. He would always be the hero. Poor Peter.

"That was an accident, and I was referring to your overbearing habit of doing exactly as you please, no matter what anyone might say."

An indefinable emotion rippled over the handsome features. "If that was true, my dearest Isa, then we would already be wed. Now, be a good girl and hush before I toss you back into the lake."

Her mouth opened to utter a sharp retort; then, noting the steely glint in his eyes, she abruptly closed it again. He was just arrogant enough to do it. She instead settled for a fierce scowl as he crossed the terrace.

As they neared the door, it was abruptly thrust

open to reveal the round, worried face of Mrs. Sculder.

"Heaven's above, what has occurred?" the cook demanded.

Barth carried Isa into the hall. "Unfortunately, Miss Lawford was tumbled into the lake."

"I feared as much would happen," Mrs. Sculder muttered in disgusted tones. "That Mr. Effinton might be bookish enough, but he knows nothing about taking care of a young lady."

Barth deliberately met Isa's flashing gaze. "My sentiments precisely."

"It was an accident," Isa wearily repeated. "Now, will you please put me down?"

"In a moment. Mrs. Sculder will you call for a hot bath?"

"At once, my lord."

"Thank you."

Flashing his most enticing smile, Barth continued down the hall and then shockingly began climbing the steps of the sweeping staircase.

"What are you doing?" she demanded.

He regarded her startled countenance as if she were a trifle dense.

"Taking you to your bedchamber so you can have a hot bath and change into some dry clothes."

"You cannot enter my bedchamber," she protested.

"Do not be a goose, Isa. I have been in your chambers on a dozen different occasions."

"When I was a child."

He lifted a deliberate brow. "Since you continue to behave as a child, then all should be well."

Her jaw tightened in an ominous manner. "I should like to . . ."

"Plant me a facer," he helpfully supplied.

"Yes."

Entering the vast rose-and-ivory bedchamber, Barth crossed toward the canopy bed. Still holding her close, he studied her pale features with a rueful smile.

"Really, Isa, you are a most ungrateful brat. Not only have I ruined my new shirt and breeches, but I have left my favorite boots standing in the mud. And all for the sake of that whey-faced milksop who has stolen my fiancée."

A peculiar tingle inched down her spine, and Isa instinctively shivered.

"I have never been your fiancée," she protested.

"Not yet." The hazel eyes abruptly darkened, and without warning, he lifted her upward to claim her mouth in a brief, searing kiss.

Isa trembled, but even as her lips treacherously parted, he was leaning forward to place her on the soft mattress. Her eyes fluttered open to discover him studying her with a disturbing intensity.

"You are shivering again, Isa. Get out of those wet clothes and I shall visit you later."

Nine

Barth was up and on his way to Cresthaven at an uncommonly early hour. In truth, he had slept precious little. It had disturbed him more than he cared to admit to have driven around the corner and discovered Isa overturned in the middle of the lake.

He had not even hesitated; he had vaulted from the still-moving carriage and sprinted toward the water. His only thought had been to reach Isa before she could be harmed.

The devil take Peter Effinton, he silently cursed as he urged his chestnut mount up the sweeping drive to the manor house. The bloody fool had nearly killed Isa. He should be locked away before he injured her further.

Not that Isa hadn't managed to take adequate care of herself, he acknowledged with a reluctant smile. Unlike most women of his acquaintance, she had not panicked, but instead had set about saving her companion from his own folly. And certainly her spirit had not been dampened by her plunge in the cold water.

His smile widened at the thought of her flashing eyes and tempting lips.

She was a most enticing brat.

How had he ever thought otherwise?

His blood stirred at the memory of their brief kiss. Lord, not even the practiced seduction of Monique had sent his heart pounding in such a manner. He could only conclude that his knowing she was determined to resist his advances made her all the more desirable.

Entering the courtyard, Barth waited for a young groom to hurry from the stables and take the reins of his horse; then, mounting the steps, he removed his hat as the door was pulled open by Rushton, and he stepped into the vaulted foyer.

"Good morning, Rushton."

The butler gave a dignified nod of his head. "Good morning, my lord."

"I am here to see Miss Lawford."

Rushton gave a regretful frown. "I fear Miss Lawford is still in her chambers, my lord."

"Good God, do not tell me that she has taken to lying abed the morning through?"

"No, sir. I believe she has developed a most unpleasant chill."

Barth's earlier annoyance with Peter Effinton rushed back with a vengeance.

"I might have suspected," he snapped; his brow furrowed in a dangerous scowl. "Blast that fumbling looby."

The faintest hint of a smile flickered over Rushton's wooden features.

"Yes, my lord."

"Has the apothecary been sent for?"

"Miss Lawford insists she has no need for Mr. Payson."

"Miss Lawford has obviously no sense when it comes to her health. Indeed, I begin to wonder if she possesses any sense at all. What female in full control of her faculties would willingly share a boat with Peter Effinton?" His expression hardened with determination. "Have a footman fetch Payson."

Rushton glanced covertly toward the staircase, clearly reluctant to disobey Isa's commands.

"My lord . . ."

Barth lifted a slender hand. "I will take responsibility, Rushton."

The butler gave a smooth bow. "Very good, Lord Wickton."

"I shall call later."

"Thank you, my lord."

Turning on his heel, Barth returned to the morning fog, but rather than heading for the stables, he instead turned toward the side path that eventually led to the enclosed kitchen garden.

Although it had been years since he had used the narrow path, he confidently slipped into the servants' entrance and made his way through the back maze of corridors. Climbing a narrow flight of stairs, he at last made his way to the main hall and the door of Isa's chambers.

It never occurred to him that he was behaving in a less than proper manner. What did he care of propriety? He was not about to leave until he had discovered for himself the status of Miss Lawford's health. And if that meant slipping into her room like a common thief to avoid any unpleasant gossip, then so be it.

With a swift glance to ensure no one was about, Barth silently pushed open the door and stepped inside.

Not surprisingly he discovered Isa lying on the bed, her golden curls haloed about her flushed countenance and her tiny frame covered by a thick blanket.

Presuming she was asleep, Barth moved directly to the bed, settling himself on the edge to study closely the disturbingly high color in her cheeks. How tiny she appeared. How fragile. As fragile as the jade figure she had proudly displayed on the table beside her bed. He would have Effinton horsewhipped if she were truly ill.

He was debating whether he should ride to Canterbury for a doctor himself or send a servant, when his thoughts were distracted as the heavy black lashes fluttered upward.

Just for a moment the amber gaze clung to his near countenance as if relieved to see him; then, abruptly, a frown of disapproval tugged at her brows.

"You," she breathed.

"Good morning, Isa."

"I suppose you bullied your way past my servants?"

Despite his concern, Barth could not help but smile at her petulant tone. With her curls in disarray and the covers pulled to her chin, she might have been a child of five rather than a grown woman.

"Your servants would have carried me to your chamber upon their shoulders if they hoped I could halt you from behaving like a stubborn fool," he informed her with a speaking glance. "However, I presumed you would prefer that we keep my rather unconventional visit between the two of us."

She gave a restless shake of her head. "What do you want?"

His hand reached out to lightly stroke her cheek, his alarm only deepening at the feel of her heated skin.

"I wished to discover for myself how you go on."

"Ghastly." She gave a decisive sneeze as if to prove her point. "Are you satisfied?"

"Of course not. I would never wish you harm, you ridiculous brat." His lips thinned. "You are hot."

Her mouth opened; then, clearly feeling too wretched to continue their delectable battle, she heaved a weary sigh.

"Yes."

A most dangerous pang clutched at Barth's heart, and he leaned toward the table next to the bed to retrieve a cloth soaking in cool water.

With a gentle tenderness, he bathed her heated features.

"Here."

Her restless motions halted beneath his soothing ministrations.

"Thank you."

"I have sent for Mr. Payson," he informed her without apology, not surprised when her tiny nose flared with annoyance.

"There was no need."

"There was every need. Indeed, I have every intention of sending to Canterbury for a doctor."

"Absurd. I have a chill, nothing more."

His expression assured her that she would have little say in the matter.

"We shall see what Payson has to say."

"Fine." She eyed him sourly. "Now that you have once again thrust your way into my presence and run roughshod over my desires, there is obviously nothing left here for you to do. Go meddle in some other unfortunate maiden's life."

He gave a husky chuckle. "How did I ever think you to be a sweet, biddable creature?"

"You more than likely had me confused with some other maiden," she said dryly; then, as another sneeze wracked her body, she gave a miserable shake of her head. "Go away."

"Poor Isa," he murmured, continuing to stroke her brow. "You do feel beastly."

The maiden briefly closed her eyes; then, as it became apparent that Barth was not yet prepared to leave, she reluctantly opened them again.

"How is Peter?"

"I haven't the least notion, nor do I care," he informed her. "Although I have often found that such bumbling fools, while creating havoc in those around them, rarely suffer themselves."

"It was not Peter's fault," she protested. "He did

not even wish to be in the boat. I convinced him that I desired a picnic on the island."

Barth carefully hid his flare of annoyance at her confession. An intimate picnic for two? The sooner he rid himself of Peter Effinton, the better.

"And you label me the bully, Isa?" He tapped the end of her nose. "Still, he should have taken greater care."

"As you would have, I suppose?"

"But of course. I do not make a habit of tipping young ladies in the lake. When I take you for a picnic, you may depend on remaining quite unharmed."

Her chin jutted. "I will not be going on a picnic with you."

"Certainly not in the next few days," he agreed.

"Not ever."

His lips curved in a small smile. "We shall see."

Her eyes once again fluttered, but this time there was no combating the feverish sleep.

"I am so tired," she muttered.

Barth's smile faded as he gazed down at the drawn features. He once again experienced that odd pain in the center of his heart.

What if it were more than a chill?

What if her lungs became inflamed? Or if the fever became worse?

Certainly a doctor must be sent for, he decided grimly.

Nothing was going to happen to Isa.

Not while he was near.

"Rest easy, my dear," he whispered, gently stroking her brow. "I shall keep you safe."

* * *

It was nearly three days before Isa felt strong enough to sit upright in bed. Although she was still weak from her prolonged fever, she was relieved to discover that her head had halted its spinning and her stomach no longer threatened to revolt at even the tiniest sip of water. Indeed, she had managed to consume a small bowl of gruel less than an hour before. Now she considered how she could possibly pass the day.

She had no desire to send for her mother. Although Mrs. Lawford meant well, her habit of bursting into tears whenever seeing her poor daughter laid upon her bed made Isa's head ache. Not even the assurances of the doctor that Barth had brought from Canterbury had managed to reassure her mother that Isa was not about to succumb to some dread end.

Perhaps she would call for her maid and have her bring a book from the library, she at last decided.

Debating what she was in the mood to peruse, Isa was startled by the sound of the door opening. Turning her head, she expected her mother or one of the numerous servants, but instead, it was the decidedly masculine countenance of Lord Wickton that suddenly appeared.

"Ah, you are awake," he said, a small smile of satisfaction curving at the sight of her perched upright on the bed.

Despite knowing she should be furious at his forward behavior, Isa discovered an answering smile curving her lips. She was well aware that he had spent the past few days downstairs not only providing comfort for her mother but commanding doctors to be fetched, fresh fruit acquired, and her room filled with flowers.

Besides, if she were perfectly honest, she would admit that she longed for a bit of company. After three days of her mother and the stern-faced doctor, even Barth's presence was a welcome diversion.

"Good afternoon, my lord. I suppose you used the servant's entrance?"

"Of course." Entering the room, he regarded her wan features with a glittering intensity. Isa resisted the wholly feminine urge to smooth her tumbled curls. Really, why could she not halt those ridiculous tremors of awareness whenever he entered a room? "How do you feel?"

"Much improved, thank you."

"Good, then I have a surprise." He opened the door wider, and a large ball of tan fur bounded into the room. Isa gave a gasp of delight as the cur of indiscriminate breeding gave a yelp and raced to leap upon the bed.

"Macbeth."

"The disreputable scamp was going into a decided decline without you."

Isa raised her head and flashed Barth a grateful smile.

"Mother had him banned for fear he might disturb me."

"I discovered him at a side door howling in a most piteous fashion."

"It was kind of you to bring him to me."

A rather teasing smile curved his lips at her soft tone. "Are you certain you are feeling well?"

She could not blame him for his amused suspicion. Since his return to Kent, she had maintained a brittle antagonism that was meant to keep him at arm's length. Although why she had felt it so necessary was something she had no desire to ponder upon. Now, however, her illness and his continued displays of kindness had undermined her resolve.

"Mother told me that you have spent every day below stairs."

An odd expression rippled over the handsome features. "You were very ill. Where else would I be?"

Her heart gave a sudden lurch, and she dropped her gaze to the dog, now sound asleep on her pillow.

"I did not even thank you for saving Peter."

"No, indeed." The more familiar edge of mockery returned to his voice. "As I recall, I was somehow blamed for the entire incident."

A rueful grimace wrinkled her nose. "You make me very angry."

"I did not use to. I once made you smile."

She slowly lifted her head. "That was long ago."

"Well, I shall prove that I can still amuse you."

Isa frowned as Barth left the room. What the devil was he doing? Then her frown abruptly fled as he returned, holding her half-finished canvas and box of paints. A sharp, poignant warmth flooded her heart. Suddenly, she was once again a young girl confined to her chamber, and he was the handsome hero sweeping to her rescue.

"Oh . . ."

"There, I made you smile," he said as he situated the painting on the window seat and returned to perch upon the bed.

The warmth and scent of his male body wrapped about her.

"I have never denied you can be extraordinarily charming," she said in breathy tones. "Indeed, you are far too charming for your own good."

His lips twisted with rueful amusement. "If I am so charming, then why are you not madly in love with me?"

Her stomach gave a sudden quiver. "I have told you that I desire a gentleman who is dependable, not charming."

"Are you sure you do not mistake dull with dependable?" he demanded.

There was no missing his subtle reference to Peter, and she gave a shake of her head.

"Please, Barth, I am in no mood to argue."

"Nor am I," he surprisingly agreed. His gaze stroked over her pale features. "This brings back old memories, does it not?"

"Yes."

"You look as if you are still twelve."

Absurdly shy beneath that warm gaze, Isa struggled to maintain her composure.

"I am sure I look a mess."

"You are beautiful," he murmured.

"You, sir, are a shameless liar."

He lifted his head, the slanting sunlight glinting off the golden fire in his chestnut hair.

"I will concede that you do not possess the more

full blown beauty of a Lady Moss or the exotic appeal of Mrs. Plantz." He named the two Incomparables that had taken London by storm. "But your skin is the texture of silk, your hair a tumble of sunlight, and your eyes the finest amber."

The huskiness of his voice tingled down her spine.

"Absurd."

"Your mother was a fool not to take you to London. You could have done far better than an impoverished earl."

Good lord. It was no wonder women tossed themselves at his feet, she thought as she hardened her expression.

"I am uninterested in such things."

"Yes, so I have discovered," he said wryly.

"I suppose you would prefer that I was anxious to become a countess?"

"It would certainly make my life considerably less complicated, but I must admit a grudging respect." Without warning, he reached out to stroke her silken curls from her brow. "There are precious few young maidens who would toss aside the prospect of acquiring a title."

"Maidens such as Miss Keaton?" The question tumbled out before she could halt the near-jealous accusation.

"Good lord, do not remind me."

Isa discovered her gaze clinging to the chiseled features that were so impossibly familiar.

"You shall have to find some such maiden," she reminded him.

"Perhaps." His hands moved to cup her chin, his

gaze lowering to her full mouth. "Or perhaps I shall simply kidnap you until you agree to become my bride."

She caught her breath at his outrageous daring. He was being absurd, of course. Civilized gentlemen did not kidnap maidens even if they were in dire need of a fortune. And civilized ladies certainly did not feel a thrill of excitement at the thought of being swept off in such a manner.

"Ridiculous." She shakily laughed.

"We shall see." The hazel eyes darkened as he abruptly lowered his head and claimed her lips in a possessive kiss. Weakened from her illness, Isa did not even attempt to evade his caress. In fact, her lips readily parted beneath his caress. *Why pretend?* she thought groggily. She had longed for this moment since he had stirred her slumbering passions in the garden. His touch deepened, seeking the yielding sweetness of her mouth. Isa felt his body stiffen with the same building excitement that raced through her own. Then, disappointingly, his lips were easing their enticing pressure. "Oh, yes," he whispered against her throbbing mouth, "we shall definitely see."

Ten

"And so the sword was turned aside, and rather than killing the blackguard who had stolen his bride, the brave knight instead mortally wounded the lady he loved."

Isa gave a wry shake of her head. She had heard the ghost story since she was a small child. The tragic tale of a beautiful bride stolen on her wedding day by the jealous lord and the frantic knight rushing to her rescue, only to kill her during the heated battle. It was said that she walked the cliffs at night while her doomed lover could be heard among the rocky coast, where he had thrown himself to his death. When she was young, the story had always made her tremble with delicious fright; now, with the sunshine flooding through the enclosed garden and Barth regarding her with a wicked smile, she felt nothing beyond a curious peace.

It was so very odd. Over the past week, Barth had barely left her side. Each day, he arrived just after breakfast and remained until after dinner. And while there a prickly awareness remained whenever he was near, she had slowly forgotten she wished him far away. Indeed, if she allowed herself to dwell upon the matter, she would have to admit that she awoke every morning awaiting his arrival.

It was simply a reaction to her confinement, she always hastily reassured herself. Anything was preferable to sitting on her own.

Glancing toward the nearby bench, she felt the familiar flicker of heat at the sight of Barth's masculine frame comfortably sprawled, his long, booted legs stretched out and crossed at the ankles. He was just so damnably handsome, she acknowledged. And he had been so very kind. It was little wonder she at times forgot he was the enemy.

"It is an absurd story," she at last murmured.

"It is true." He tugged at his ear in a manner that assured her that he was teasing. "I have seen her walk the cliffs at night."

"I am no longer an impressionable ten-year-old who believes in ghosts," she informed him.

He studied her pale features for a disturbing moment.

"So you fear nothing?"

She drew in a sharp breath. Of course she feared, she inwardly acknowledged. She feared having her heart broken. She feared being betrayed. And most of all, she feared the dangers of trusting in love.

"Certainly not ladies in white or long-dead knights," she forced herself to retort. "And what of you? Do you fear nothing?"

Surprisingly, a somber expression settled on the lean features.

"During the war, I discovered I feared a great number of things."

She experienced a swift pang of remorse. "I am so sorry."

The hazel gaze lingered on her softened features. "Do not be."

"What was it like?"

"War?"

"Yes."

"Cold. Dirty. And for the most part, unbearably tedious." He paused as if reliving his days with the regiment. "I do not know if I could have survived without the companionship of Philip and Simon."

"It was said that you saved a gentleman's life."

He shrugged aside her words. "We all helped one another."

"It must have been horrible."

"Yes. Quite horrible," he agreed in soft tones. "Which is why we lingered so long in Italy. We needed time to distance ourselves from the memories before returning home."

"Yes."

A rather odd smile curved his lips. "And, of course, Rome is a most fascinating location to linger."

Isa suddenly stiffened. Yes, she could just imagine what was so fascinating.

"Of course." Her smile was stiff. "I have heard the ladies are quite beautiful."

The wicked glint returned to the hazel eyes. "Perhaps, but I was referring to an old Gypsy we encountered. She gave us the oddest blessing."

"Great riches, I suppose," she quipped, not believing him for a moment.

"Actually, her blessing was that each of us would discover true love before the heat of summer burns again."

"True love?" She raised her brows. "How fortunate for you."

He chuckled. "Yes, indeed."

"Did you believe her?"

"Certainly not at the time."

"And now?"

"Now I begin to wonder what true love is." He leaned forward, close enough so that he could capture her hand in a firm grip. "Perhaps you will enlighten me."

Warmth flooded from his slender fingers through her skin and into her very blood.

"Me?"

"You must love Mr. Effinton," he retorted.

Her lashes swiftly fluttered downward to hide her all too expressive eyes.

"My feelings are private."

His thumb stroked a disturbing path over her knuckles.

"At least tell me what such a grand love entails. Does your heart stop when he enters the room? Do you long to hear the sound of his voice?" His own voice suddenly lowered. "Do you awake in the night aching for the feel of his arms about you?"

She roughly bit her bottom lip. Such sensations were not love. They were deceitful pleasures that lured a woman to behave as a perfect fool.

"That is enough."

"What is amiss, Isa?"

"I do not wish to discuss this."

"Very well," he surprisingly agreed, his tone edged with amusement. "Shall I tell you another ghost story?"

She abruptly lifted her gaze to stab him with an unwavering intensity.

"Why are you here?"

His free hand lifted, lightly brushing her pale cheek.

"Where else would I be?"

She trembled but refused to allow her gaze to falter. "London."

"I am in no hurry to return." His fingers firmly cupped her chin. "Besides, I could not leave while you were ill."

Those delicious tingles once more raced through her body. Dangerous, unwelcome tingles.

"I am no concern of yours."

"I believe that we have already established that I am your friend."

She did not believe him for a moment. She was all too aware of his necessity to wed a large dowry and to do so swiftly.

"And you still believe that I will marry you?"

He abruptly pulled away and regarded her with a narrowed gaze. Ridiculously, Isa felt a pang of regret at the loss of his warm touch.

"You think I am only pretending concern out of some devious hope to acquire your dowry?"

There was an edge in his tone that warned her that

she had somehow managed to stir his normally placid temper. She discovered herself reluctant to openly confront him with her inner suspicions.

"I do not know what I think."

"My concern for you is very real, Isa."

It would be easy to believe him, she conceded. No one could have been more attentive to her needs or more patient as she slowly convalesced. Indeed, he had been her most faithful visitor. Unlike Peter, who had not even bothered to call.

Still, it was all so very convenient. Would he be at her side if he had no need of her dowry?

"I have no reason to trust you."

There was a short pause before Barth heaved an audible sigh.

"Perhaps not. I have behaved as a selfish boor and treated you with an indifference you did not deserve," he slowly admitted, making her lift her gaze in startled disbelief. "But that was only because I resented being forced into marriage. I desired to forget my obligations for a short time."

She gave an unconscious flinch. Forced into marriage? *The devil take him.* Did he think any maiden would wish a bridegroom who was being forced to the altar?

"Very flattering," she muttered.

"I am attempting to be honest with you."

"There is no need."

"There is every need." He once again reached out to grasp her hand. "I believe we could deal quite well together."

"Absurd."

"Why?" He leaned forward, the scent of his soap mixing with the budding daffodils. "We have much in common. We were once great friends. And not even you can deny that there is a potent attraction between us."

Her eyes abruptly darkened. No, she could not deny the attraction. How could she when she trembled at his every touch? She had been attracted to the gentleman for as long as she could recall. But that was not enough.

"I do not love you," she denied in tones perhaps a bit more fierce than necessary.

His hand tightened on her fingers, his lean features determined.

"But you desire me."

"No."

A sudden tension entered the garden as a flare of heat glittered in the hazel eyes. It was obvious she had challenged his pride. Her own heart faltered as he slowly leaned forward.

"Shall I prove it, Isa?" he demanded, his gaze deliberately lowering to her parted lips.

"Barth."

With breathless anticipation, she awaited the persuasive seduction of his kiss, only to abruptly freeze as the sound of raised voices floated through the air.

"Sir, I beg of you . . ." her butler protested in outrage.

Cursing the flare of regret at the interruption, Isa drew away from Barth. Was she forever doomed to react like a moonling whenever he was near?

With an effort, she smoothed her curls and straightened her shoulders. She should be deeply relieved at the timely interruption, she sternly assured herself.

"Out of my way, you starched-up peacock," a familiar male voice rumbled in annoyance.

Isa felt a surge of pleased surprise as she recognized the voice of her grandfather. In all her days she could not recall his visiting Cresthaven. She could not imagine what had brought him at such an opportune moment. "But Miss Lawford is entertaining," Rushton said, futilely attempting to halt the determined gentleman.

The servant might as well have saved his breath.

"Aye, and I not be good enough for the likes of the local nobs," Edward Brunston charged. "Well, I ain't leaving until I've seen my granddaughter, so you might as well step aside."

"Sir . . ." Rushton gave a last protest before Edward was sweeping past him and into the garden.

Both Isa and Barth rose to their feet as the large, florid-faced man with silver hair and piercing blue eyes came into view.

"Grandfather." Isa smiled, and stepping forward, she was pulled into a strong embrace.

Edward at last stepped back, regarding her pleased expression with a frown.

"Why did you miss our appointment?" he demanded bluntly.

Appointment? Isa gave a sudden gasp. How could she possibly have forgotten what day it was? She had been meeting her grandfather on this date every month since she was a child. It was his way of being a part of her life without intruding into what he termed her "proper" world.

She had always looked forward to their luncheon at the local inn, their long drives through the countryside, or pots of tea in a private parlor when the weather was bad.

Good lord, she must be growing soft in the noodle to have lost track of her days, she chastised herself in disgust.

"Forgive me, Grandfather," she murmured with genuine regret. "I completely forgot."

A speculative glint entered the blue eyes. "I feared something had happened to you."

Knowing that the wily old man was bound to be suspicious of her odd lapse, Isa readily grasped onto the most convenient excuse.

"I was ill, but I am much improved now."

Predictably, the speculative glance became one of concern. "You are pale."

"I am fine."

"She is still in need of rest," a darkly masculine voice intruded as Barth moved to stand close at her side.

Isa swallowed a sigh. She should have suspected that he would not remain meekly in the background.

"Grandfather, may I introduce Lord Wickton? Lord Wickton, my grandfather, Mr. Brunston."

The bushy gray brows lowered another notch as her grandfather subjected Barth to a thorough survey.

"Wickton, eh?"

With a natural elegance, Barth gave a slight bow. "A pleasure, Mr. Brunston."

"No, it ain't," Edward retorted in his blunt style. "A gentleman can't wish to be encroached upon. Wouldn't have come if I hadn't been worried about my favorite lass."

Isa tilted her chin. When it came to her beloved grandfather, she did not care a whit what others might think. Including Barth.

"I am glad you did come," she insisted.

"No, no. Your mother is right. Wouldn't do to have me popping up. Much better to meet at the inn."

"Nonsense," Isa denied. "What do I care what the neighbors may say? You are far more important than any gossip."

"You are a good lass." Her grandfather patted her cheek with a smile. "Now, what has made you look so pale?"

Isa shrugged. "A mere chill."

Barth once again intruded. "She was quite ill."

She flashed him an exasperated frown. "I am much improved."

"Has a doctor been sent for?" Edward demanded.

"Yes," Isa hurriedly agreed, knowing her grandfather was quite capable of calling in every doctor throughout England.

"He insisted that she must rest." Barth met her glittering gaze squarely. "And that she keep warm."

"I am fine," Isa insisted.

Barth turned to the older man, who was regarding them closely.

"Has she always been so stubborn?"

"Aye." Edward gave a chuckle. "A heart of gold and a will of iron."

Traitor, Isa thought with a stab of annoyance.

"Do you mind?"

Edward patted her cheek again. "I should be on my way."

"Could you not stay?" Barth surprisingly insisted.

"I only came to see about Isa."

"She would no doubt feel much happier after a visit with her grandfather. And she is still too weak to travel to the inn."

A hint of pleased color crept beneath Edward's cheeks as Barth wove his potent charm. It seemed not even the hardheaded businessman was immune.

"I should not like to intrude."

"I assure you that I am the intruder, eh, Isa?" Barth teased with a knowing smile.

With a wry grimace, she turned her attention to her grandfather.

"Please stay, Grandfather."

"Well . . ."

With a firm stride, Barth crossed toward the open French doors, where the butler still anxiously hovered.

"Rushton, see to tea, will you? And tell Mr. Brunston's groom to take the horses to the stables."

Keeping his dismay well hidden, the butler offered a stiff bow.

"At once, my lord."

Edward regarded the younger gentleman with a stern eye before giving a sharp laugh.

"By gad, Isa, I do believe you have at last met your match."

Eleven

It was several hours later when Isa walked her grandfather back to his waiting carriage. Surprisingly, the afternoon had been a success. Due in most part to Barth's gracious manners, she reluctantly acknowledged. He had treated Edward Brunston with genuine respect. Not once had he displayed any airs of condescension or patronage.

Indeed, he had even revealed a shrewd interest in the numerous businesses that Edward owned throughout England. Within a few moments, her grandfather had lost his self-conscious unease at being in the company of an aristocrat and conversed with an open friendliness that revealed his own regard for the nobleman.

Isa had found herself quietly amazed at the mutual affinity. Her grandfather had always professed a cynical disregard for worthless dandies, while Barth's position demanded he treat a mere businessman with a measure of distaste. But neither had revealed any hint of their differing stations. Isa had also been amazed by Barth's seeming ability to sense that she wished for time alone with her grandfather. After sharing tea, he had risen and offered them wishes for a pleasant visit before making his farewell.

For the remainder of the afternoon, Isa had chatted inanely, determinedly keeping her grandfather from probing too deeply into her private affairs.

Of course, it was a wasted effort. As they reached the glossy black carriage, her grandfather firmly tilted her countenance upward for a piercing inspection.

"What is it, lass?" he demanded.

"What do you mean?"

"There is more than a lingering chill that is making you so pale and drawn."

Isa grimaced, realizing that she could not deceive Edward Brunston.

"I have told Mother that I will not wed Lord Wickton," she reluctantly confessed.

"Ah. And that is what is causing your sleepless nights?"

"Of course not," she hastily denied. *Botheration.* Did he have to be so perceptive? She did not wish anyone to know the restless hours she laid awake, struggling to deny the empty ache in the middle of her heart. "I am quite satisfied with my decision."

There was a pause before a rather mysterious smile curved his lips.

"He is a fine gentleman. I liked him."

Of course, Isa concurred wryly. There was no one in all of England who did not like Barth Juston, earl of Wickton.

"He is a shameless rake," she informed him in stern tones.

"Is he?" The shaggy brows raised.

"Yes."

"Are you certain that you do not mistake being a hardened rake with the natural curiosities of youth?"

Her tiny features settled in lines of distaste. She doubted that Barth's beautiful and sophisticated mistress would wish to be considered no more than a curiosity of youth.

"He is just like Father."

"No." Edward gave a decisive shake of his head. "Your father is a weak man with a deplorable lack of morals. Lord Wickton is certainly not weak, and from all accounts he is considered an honorable gentleman."

An unconscious pain flared through her amber eyes. "Hardly honorable."

"Why do you say that?"

"He has a beautiful mistress in London."

"Does he?" Edward shrugged, his smile widening. "It is hardly uncommon, my dear. Most young gentlemen acquire a mistress before they wed. Besides, I would wager that he does not gaze at her with such longing."

"What?"

"I may be old, but I am not without eyes."

Her breath caught somewhere in her throat. Barth gazed at her with longing? No. It was too ridiculous.

"Lord Wickton has no interest in me beyond my dowry," she said stiffly.

Edward gave a soft laugh. "It is not a dowry he is thinking of when he looks upon you."

"Absurd."

"You are a good lass. Do not let your stubborn pride steal your chance for happiness."

Had he not listened to a word she had been saying?

"This has nothing to do with my pride."

"Does it not?" her grandfather demanded. "Are you certain that you are not trying to convince your-self that Lord Wickton is like your father rather than admit he wounded your heart by leaving Kent?"

Her face paled at the accusation.

"That is ridiculous."

"Is it? When you were young, you placed him on a very high pedestal, my love. He was bound to topple off someday. Don't be too hard on him. He is just a man."

"A man I no longer trust."

"Perhaps it is your heart that you no longer trust." He reached up to lightly tap her nose. "Think upon what I have said. We will meet again next month."

After yet another fitful night, Isa rose early and determinedly dressed in a sturdy gown of mint green and golden pelisse. Then, avoiding the breakfast room where her mother was certain to be enjoying her coffee, she slipped out through the door and into the courtyard.

She had no desire to explain her need for the fresh spring air or her determination to avoid Barth's daily visit. She did not even wish to dwell on the reasons herself. All she allowed herself to ponder was a sudden urge to speak with Peter Effinton.

With a brisk step, she crossed the cobblestones and entered the narrow path that wound its way toward the vicarage and into the nearby village. About her, the smell of sweet clover hung in the air, and in the distance the sound of water rushing over the rocks echoed from the cliffs.

She slowed her step and forced herself to enjoy the warmth of the sun and the play of butterflies over the newly budded wildflowers. It was the first occasion she had left the estate since her tumble into the lake. She should at least make the effort to enjoy her newfound freedom.

Long minutes later, she skirted the small stone church and entered the gardens surrounding the vicarage. As expected, Peter was just leaving for his morning stroll as she approached. He was nearly upon her before he noticed her presence, and with a muffled exclamation, the young gentleman stumbled to a surprised halt.

"Oh."

Isa allowed her gaze to drift over the ill-fitted coat and breeches stained with spots of ink. A familiar stab of amused fondness rushed through her heart. She did care a great deal for this man. He was kind, intelligent, and utterly predictable. Precisely the qualities she desired in a gentleman.

So why, then, had a dark cloud of doubt begun to hang about her head?

Blast Lord Wickton and his disturbing insinuations, she inwardly sighed.

"Good morning, Peter."

"Isa. How are you?"

"I am well."

"Good. I had heard . . ." He gave a rather awkward cough. "It was said that Lord Wickton sent to Canterbury for a doctor."

Isa tried not to consider the realization that Peter would never have gone to such an effort.

"Yes, he did."

"I was quite concerned."

She stepped closer, an unconscious frown marring her brow. "Were you?"

"Yes, of course."

"I thought you might call," she said softly.

"Well . . ." He gave another awkward cough. "I did not wish to disturb you."

A treacherous suspicion that it was more a dislike at being near an invalid than fear of disturbing her was swiftly banished.

Blast Lord Wickton.

"You are always welcome at Cresthaven."

A faint blush touched his cheeks. "Very kind of you, Isa."

"I trust that you did not suffer from our dunking?"

"No." He gave a shake of his head. "Never sick, you know."

"Good."

A small silence fell as he shifted beneath her steady regard. Then a sudden light entered his eyes.

"I have uncovered a most fascinating manuscript. Would you like to see it?"

Isa felt a pang of disappointment. Clearly, Peter

had not been burdened too heavily with concern for her welfare if he could devote his attentions to continuing his research.

"Not today, thank you."

He appeared once again at a loss.

"Perhaps we could just sit and talk?"

"Why, yes."

Together they moved toward the small bench that faced the nearby road. It was so narrow that they were forced to sit close together, but Isa felt none of the unnerving tingles in the pit of her stomach that Barth created.

Of which she was quite relieved, she tried to tell herself.

"It is a most beautiful day," she said with a small smile.

"Ah . . ." Peter glanced about as if noting the mild spring weather for the first time. "So it is."

Taking a moment to consider her words, Isa turned the conversation toward the subject that had been plaguing her for the past few days.

Barth was wrong about Peter, and she would prove it.

"I believe that Miss Keaton has left Kent."

Peter appeared unconcerned. "Has she?"

"Did you have the opportunity to speak with her?"

"No." He gave a vague shrug. "Not really."

"You were once very close," she prompted.

"Well, we were both young."

"But you must have cared for her?"

"I suppose."

Isa tried not to be disturbed by his lack of emotion.

It had been long ago. And not all people allowed the pangs of first love to continually disrupt their lives.

"It is fortunate that you did not wed."

"Yes, we had nothing in common."

She carefully regarded his pale features. "No doubt, if you do decide to marry, you will choose a lady who shares your interests?"

A startled expression rippled over his countenance, as if the notion of marriage had never even entered his head. Then a slowly dawning smile curved his lips.

"Yes. Yes, indeed," he agreed. "It should be lovely to have someone to transcribe my notes and help with my research."

Isa's heart faltered at the impetuous words. "That sounds more like a secretary than a wife," she protested.

"Well, she would also care for the house and see to the cooking."

"Surely that is not all you would seek in a wife?"

His brow wrinkled with thought. "I suppose she would have to be a restful sort. I am far too busy to be bothered with a great deal of fuss. And someone who would realize the importance of my work and help tend to the daily matters so that I could concentrate on my research."

His tone warmed as the pleasant image of being devotedly coddled formed in his mind even as Isa felt herself grow cold. She was uncertain what she had hoped to hear. She had always known that Peter was not overly romantic or poetic in nature. She had even admired his single-minded obsession with his studies.

But while she did not expect passionate confessions of what he desired in a wife, she had not thought even Peter could be quite so self-absorbed. For goodness' sake, he could hardly expect a woman to be satisfied with keeping his notes in order and his stomach full.

What of love?

"That sounds lovely," she muttered.

Unaware of her darkened eyes and faint droop of her lips, Peter gave a decisive nod of his head.

"My mother was a great help to my father."

"Was she?"

"She helped with his sermons and visited the poor. And of course she ensured that he was not interrupted when he was occupied with his studies. That should be quite convenient for a gentleman."

"Yes."

The sound of approaching horses rumbled through the air, and it was with a decided sense of relief that Isa turned toward the road.

She had not wanted to believe Barth's accusation that a wife would claim but a small token of Peter's attention. Even though she had no doubt suspected the truth all along. Instead, she had tried to convince herself that the young man would eventually grow attached to her and become the suitor she thought she wanted.

Oddly, though, the realization that Peter would never be the husband she had envisioned caused no more than a twinge of regret. Surely she should be devastated by the truth. After all, she had devoted months to the dream of sharing a small cottage with the young scholar. She had even invented two children and a tiny puppy that would lie on the stoop. Why wasn't her heart broken as it had been when Barth had betrayed her?

Lost in her thoughts, Isa vaguely watched the approaching curricle. It was not until a lithe form vaulted onto the street and then firmly marched into the garden that she was aware of her danger.

Her musings abruptly vanished as she met the glittering hazel gaze of Lord Wickton. Whatever her changing feelings for Peter, nothing had altered her determination not to be bullied, cajoled, or seduced into marriage with Barth. She would rather be on her own.

"There you are." Barth advanced at a relentless pace.

She smiled wryly, having no doubt he had been searching the countryside for her. He was nothing if not determined.

Peter belatedly rose to his feet and offered a bow. "Good morning, my lord."

Barth ignored him as he regarded Isa's defiant expression with a narrowed gaze.

"What are you doing?"

"Simply enjoying a pleasant conversation with Peter," she retorted.

He was not appeased; indeed, there was an uncharacteristic harshness to his handsome features.

"The doctor said you were not to overtire yourself."

"I am not in the least tired."

"He also said that you were to remain out of the wind."

"For goodness' sake, Barth, there is not a hint of wind," she exclaimed in exasperation.

"I am certain that Mr. Effinton would agree that you should not be taking unnecessary risks with your health."

Predictably, Peter was swift to agree. "Certainly not."

"I am not tired, and there is no wind, so if that is all . . ."

"Very well. Since you are confident there is no danger, perhaps you would join me for a drive?" he smoothly interrupted.

She briefly wondered if anyone had ever told this man no.

"Peter was just about to show me his latest research," she readily lied.

"Well, we can discuss this later," Peter insisted.

A sudden, worrisome smile softened Barth's features.

"An excellent notion," he announced. "Perhaps over dinner. I have two guests arriving, and I hope you both will join us for dinner."

Isa stiffened with a flare of suspicion. "More guests, my lord?"

That devilish glint returned to his eyes. "Yes."

"You have quite enlivened our dull neighborhood."

He gave a slight, mocking bow. "Thank you."

He was plotting something, she told herself. Something devious.

"More relatives?" she demanded.

His lips twitched at her direct thrust. "No. Indeed, Mr. Effinton might be familiar with one or two of my acquaintances."

"Me?" Peter regarded Lord Wickton in confusion. "I fear that I know few people in London."

"I believe that both Sir Wilhelm and Mr. Brockfield have lectured at Oxford."

There was a loud gasp as Peter took a stumbling step forward.

"You . . . You cannot mean to say they will be in Kent?"

"Yes."

"But that is most wonderful," Peter breathed, a decided glow on his thin face.

"Then you are acquainted with them?"

"By reputation only." Peter was nearly stammering in his excitement. Isa had never seen him so eager. "To think that I will meet with them . . . speak with them. But they cannot wish to meet me."

Isa's suspicions deepened as she watched Barth's lips twitch with amusement. He had obviously expected Peter's reaction. No doubt he had even depended upon it, she realized with a flash of insight. He had failed to come between her and Peter with Miss Keaton, so now he was using a far more potent weapon.

Scholars.

The devious toad.

"I assure you that they will be delighted to speak with so worthy a scholar."

Peter flushed with pleasure even as he gave a shake of his head.

"No, I am lowly indeed in comparison."

"But you will come?" Barth pressed.

"I should be honored." Peter choked. "Quite, quite honored."

Barth smiled. "Good."

"I must gather my notes," Peter abruptly announced, then, with an afterthought, offered his benefactor a deep bow. "Thank you, my lord, thank you."

Without so much as a glance toward Isa, Peter turned and hurried back toward the house. Isa had no doubt that in his excitement he had forgotten her very existence. Still, it was toward the gentleman currently regarding her with an annoyingly satisfied expression that she directed her anger.

How dared he dangle respected scholars beneath Peter's nose? It was no better than a common bribe.

"Well, it appears that you are now free to join me for a drive," he drawled.

Her eyes narrowed to dangerous slits. "Tell me, my lord, is there nothing you will not do to achieve your desires?"

Without warning, he stepped forward and cupped her chin in a firm grasp.

"Nothing, Isa," he informed her in a disturbingly relentless tone. "Nothing at all."

Twelve

Although the spring was mild, a fire burned in the vast fireplace. It helped to dispel the gloom of the formal salon, and Barth glanced about the room with an unusual sense of satisfaction. Of course, if he were perfectly honest, he would acknowledge that his contentment stemmed less from the stiff setting and more from the sight of the three gentleman standing in a far corner, deeply involved in conversation.

Since Peter's arrival earlier this evening, he had been thoroughly taken with Sir Wilhelm and Mr. Brockfield. He had barely acknowledged Isa's arrival and had all but ignored her during dinner.

Barth allowed a wry smile to curve his lips. He, on the other hand, had been unable to keep his gaze off the lovely maiden attired in an ivory satin gown with seed pearls stitched onto the hem. She appeared as fresh and innocent as a newly budded rose. A most enticing rose, he thought with a tingle of awareness.

How any gentleman could prefer to devote his attention to the gaunt, silver-haired Sir Wilhelm and the younger, dark-haired Mr. Brockfield defied comprehension. He could only presume that Peter Effington was a bit addlepated.

Turning slightly, Barth viewed his mother stiffly conversing with Mrs. Lawford; then, turning further, his gaze at last landed upon Isa, seated alone on a brocade sofa.

An unconsciously possessive expression settled on his countenance as he studied her delicate profile.

How beautiful she was, he acknowledged with an odd pang. But even as he marveled at her loveliness, he could not deny there was a hint of pallor to her skin and that she had not yet regained the weight she had lost during her illness.

She was clearly not taking proper care of herself, he thought with a flare of disapproval. His mouth firmed with determination. Once she was his wife, he would ensure that she was kept utterly safe.

Strangely, it never occurred to him that he had never before been so aware of another's well-being. His mother had never encouraged him to be particularly close, and his friends were capable of seeing to their own needs. As for his mistresses, they had always been careful not to make demands upon his heart.

Now he found his feet impulsively taking him toward the woman who had begun to dominate his every thought. Without regard to her icy glare, he settled close beside her, delighted by the revealing shiver that shook her body as his leg pressed intimately to her own.

"Isa," he murmured with a teasing smile. "All alone?"

Not surprisingly, she met his gaze with a tilt of her

chin. Despite his earlier imaginings, this was one woman he would never dominate.

"It was what you wanted, was it not?"

He attempted to appear innocent. "I merely invited my friends to enjoy a few days at Graystone."

"What odd friends you possess, my lord," she gritted, not believing him for a moment. "A maiden from Dover who just happens to have been engaged to Peter and now two notable scholars whom Peter has long admired."

"I possess many friends," he informed her with a small shrug of his shoulders.

The ice melted as a flare of anger glowed in the amber eyes.

"You brought them here to once again create trouble between me and Peter."

He paused for a moment to carefully consider his words.

"I will admit that I desired you to realize that you will never come first in Mr. Effinton's affections."

A strange, unreadable emotion rippled over her delicate features before she swiftly regained control of herself.

"I do not know what you mean."

Really, was the chit being deliberately blind? he wondered in exasperation.

"Tell me, Isa, has Mr. Effinton spoken with you once this evening?"

It was her turn to shrug. "He is naturally overwhelmed by meeting Sir Wilhelm and Mr. Brockfield."

"So overwhelmed that he has not even noted how

exceptionally beautiful you appear?" He deliberately lowered his gaze to the provocative cut of her bodice. "Surely a new gown is deserving of a compliment or two?"

She stiffened and attempted to pull away, but the confines of the sofa gave her little room.

"Peter does not possess your sophistication or your experience with women," she informed him in strained tones. "Which is precisely what I admire most about him."

He smiled with dry humor as the thrust slid home. As a well-trained fencer, he knew when he left himself open to a killing hit. Still, he refused to concede that she was as indifferent to the snubbing as she pretended. What woman would be if she truly cared about a gentleman?

"So it does not bother you to be left neglected in the corner?"

Her gaze dropped to the hands clenched in her lap. "I do not need to have a gentleman dancing constant attendance upon me."

"That is odd."

"What?"

"I thought it was because you felt I had neglected you that I was thrown over."

Her head abruptly lifted at his accusation, her eyes stormy.

"One evening can hardly compare with five years. And it was far more than mere neglect that convinced me that we were unsuited."

"Of course, you had decided I was an incurable rogue," he supplied in dry tones.

She drew in a sharp breath. "Must we discuss this yet again?"

His smile faded as he leaned forward. Only the knowledge that his mother and Mrs. Lawford were bound to be watching them with anxious concern kept him from grasping her tiny face in his hands.

"I just wish to know if you thought that I would be unfaithful once we were married."

Her eyes darkened with pain at his blunt question. "Barth, now is hardly an appropriate moment—"

"Just answer the question, Isa."

"Why?" Her lips trembled before she pressed them to a thin line. "You would hardly admit that you planned to keep a mistress after our marriage."

An unexplainable pain twisted his heart at her bitter words. Did she truly believe that he could be so lacking in character?

"Tell me, Isa, did you expect me to stash this mistress in the village? Or perhaps you thought I would simply install her at Graystone?"

Her cheeks reddened, but she refused to give sway.

"I believe most gentlemen are clever enough to maintain a separate establishment in London."

He refused to consider the elegant establishment he had so recently given up. It all seemed another life. One that was swiftly fading from memory.

"Whether you choose to believe me or not, Isa, it has never been my intention to be unfaithful to my wife."

"As I said, you would hardly admit it if you were."

"I am not in the habit of lying."

For long moments their gazes battled as if she

sought the truth deep in his eyes; then she gave a sharp shake of her head.

"This is a ridiculous conversation."

Barth wisely suppressed the urge to continue the argument. He had at least made her consider the possibility that she had judged him too harshly.

"Very well," he conceded. "Then I shall instead tell you that I enjoyed meeting your grandfather."

Caught off guard by his abrupt change in conversation, her expression softened. It had taken little wit for him to realize she was decidedly attached to Mr. Brunston. And that she was highly sensitive to the least hint of insult toward his lack of social position.

"You were very gracious to him," she reluctantly conceded.

"Why should I not be?"

She gave a faint grimace as she pointedly glanced toward the coldly perfect Lady Wickton.

"I doubt that your mother would be pleased at the notion you had made the acquaintance of a shop-keeper."

"My mother is a ghastly snob," he readily admitted. "I am not."

"No," she agreed.

Barth pressed home his advantage. "Why should I not admire a gentleman who has managed to make such a success of his life?"

A small smile touched her lovely countenance. "He is quite remarkable."

"You are a great deal like him."

Isa appeared startled by his comparison. "Me?"

"Yes. Strong, honorable, and quite unable to sway once you have set your mind."

She could not prevent a sudden laugh. "Meaning that I am stubborn?"

Although she was always lovely, there was a luminous beauty to her features when she laughed. Barth had a sudden desire to always see her smiling.

"Do you recall when we were young and you realized that the schoolmaster refused to teach the girls in the village to read?" he asked gently.

"He said it would make them think that they were above their station." She gave a disgusted shake of her head. "Ridiculous man."

Barth recalled the golden-haired child that had resolutely faced the furious schoolmaster with a calm dignity.

"You threatened to have your father use his influence to have him removed from his position."

"He could have not known that my father would never have made the effort," she said dryly.

"You also sat in the school every morning to ensure that he did not frighten the girls away."

"I fear that few came."

He studied her for a long moment, recognizing that he had never encountered another woman who would have done what Isa had done. It had taken more than mere courage. It had taken a heart kind enough to risk gossip and ridicule rather than turn a blind eye, as everyone else had done.

"But you refused to be intimidated, and you did not care that the boys laughed at your efforts. You knew what was right and were willing to fight for your beliefs."

She appeared thrown off guard by the sincerity in his tone.

"It was hardly a fight."

His gaze stroked over her pale features. "It was quite heroic."

She frowned in discomfort, uneasy at his compliments. "I am surprised you even recall such a trivial incident."

He grimaced with a stab of remorse—an unwelcome sensation that occurred all too frequently in Isa's company.

"I remember a great deal, although I am just beginning to realize that I have too long taken your special qualities for granted."

"Nonsense," she protested in embarrassment.

He refused to be put off. "It is not nonsense. You have always been kind and brave and trustworthy. Precisely the qualities any gentleman would seek in a bride."

She seemed to catch her breath at his low words; then her long lashes were fluttering downward to hide her expressive eyes.

"You are very good at this," she muttered.

"At what?"

"Seducing a woman."

A swift, fiercely pleasurable flame of heat flicked through his blood. Damn but he wanted this woman. What would she do if he were to lift her in his arms and carry her upstairs to his bed?

"I should very much like to seduce you, Isa," he murmured in husky tones.

He watched with delight as the color rushed to, then faded from, her tiny countenance. She was far from indifferent to him, as much as she might wish to deny the truth.

Briefly wondering if he could convince her to take a stroll through the garden so that he could at least pull her into his arms and relieve his growing desire with a kiss, Barth was distracted by the determined wave of Andrew Brockfield from across the room.

"Wickton," he called in imperious tones.

Barth smothered the instinctive stab of annoyance at the interruption. There was already a speculative expression on Andrew's handsome features as he noted Barth's intimate seclusion with Isa. Instead, he smoothed his countenance to an unreadable mask.

"Yes?"

"We are having an argument on the import of Greek culture on Roman civilization. You must come and settle the issue."

Realizing that he had no choice but to join his guests, Barth reluctantly rose to his feet, but as Isa raised her head with obvious relief, he flashed her a warning gaze.

"We will continue this later."

Several hours later, Barth poured a brandy for himself and Andrew. Crossing the library, he handed the glass to the seated gentleman and tossed his own frame into the matching wing chair flanking the smoldering fireplace.

His mother and Sir Wilhelm had excused themselves after the guests had taken their leave, but with a determined air, Barth had requested that Andrew join him for a last drink.

Now he regarded his companion with a narrowed gaze. "Well?"

Sipping the amber liquid, Andrew raised his brows. "Yes?"

"What do you think?"

"I think that she is lovely."

Barth gave a sharp laugh at his friend's perception. "I am not speaking of Miss Lawford."

Andrew gave a mock sigh. "A pity. She has a most engaging smile."

Barth steered the conversation toward his goal. "I am referring to Mr. Effinton."

"Ah."

"He is reputed to be a budding scholar."

"I should have suspected that I was not invited here to simply enjoy the fine Kent countryside."

Barth smiled. "You are always welcome at Graystone, Andrew."

"Does that include becoming better acquainted with the beautiful Miss Lawford?" Andrew demanded in sly tones.

Although Barth's smile remained intact, there was no missing the sudden flare in his eyes.

"Absolutely not."

Andrew gave a small laugh. "Very well, Wickton, what is it that you wish to know?"

"Just your impression of Mr. Effinton."

Andrew settled himself more comfortably in the chair. "Actually, I have read a paper of his."

"Really?"

"Yes. I was lecturing at Oxford, and his teacher requested that I review his work."

It had been at Oxford when Barth had first met Andrew. Although Andrew was older and considerably more studious than Barth, they had struck up a close friendship. He had also introduced Sir Wilhelm, who had once harbored a violent tendre for Lady Sarah. Barth had known he could depend upon the two of them to aid him in his plot.

"And?"

"And I found his research to be near brilliant."

"How intriguing," Barth murmured.

"Unfortunately, he was without the funds or necessary connections to continue his education. I always considered it a great pity."

"Yes," Barth agreed. "A great pity."

Andrew slowly set aside his glass. "What is your interest in the young gentleman?"

"Ah . . . that is rather a delicate situation."

"I do not suppose this delicate situation has anything to do with Miss Lawford?"

Barth's lips twitched. "Now, why would you suppose that?"

"Because I could not help but notice the particular attention you were paying her this evening. Or the fact that she seemed less than delighted by such attentions."

Barth abruptly drained the brandy, grimacing as the fiery spirit slid down his throat.

"You are very observant."

"Yes, I am," Andrew agreed with a piercing gaze.

It was obvious he would have to confess the truth, he reluctantly allowed. Despite his pride he needed this man's help.

"It has long been expected that Miss Lawford and I would wed. Unfortunately, while I was absent from Kent, she convinced herself that I am not to be trusted."

Andrew seemed unsurprised. "And?"

"And that Mr. Effinton would be a far more dependable husband."

"Ah."

"A ridiculous notion, of course."

"Is it?"

Barth's features hardened. "Yes."

Andrew paused for a long moment. "What is it that you want from me?"

"I wish you to use your influence to find an appropriate post where his brilliant mind will not be wasted."

"And one that is far from Kent?" Andrew concluded, swift to grasp Barth's meaning.

"But of course."

"It seems rather devious," Andrew pointed out in soft tones.

Barth gave a small shrug. "You said yourself that it would be a shame to waste such talents."

"Yes. Although Mr. Effinton may not be eager to leave Kent if he possesses feelings for Miss Lawford."

"At the moment, Mr. Effinton possesses feelings for nothing beyond his own studies. Something I very much intend to encourage."

Andrew pursed his lips. "I suppose if he does not desire to pursue a career away from Kent, then he could always refuse my offer. After all, he is not in desperate need of employment."

"Then you will help?"

There was another pause as Andrew considered the request. Barth remained silent, unwilling to press his friend. At last, Andrew gave a slow nod of his head.

"Very well. When we leave, I will ask Mr. Effinton to accompany me as my secretary. He will no doubt be anxious to travel with me to Brussels."

Barth breathed out a sigh of relief. At last he was to be rid of the pesky young man.

"I knew you would not fail me," he congratulated his companion.

Andrew lifted his brows. "That does not assure you Miss Lawford will become your wife."

A slow, decidedly predatory smile touched Barth's mouth.

"You can safely leave Miss Lawford in my hands."

Thirteen

Isa was in a decided muddle.

The man was impossible, of course.

Utterly impossible.

First, he had deliberately attempted to lure Peter away with the annoying Miss Keaton. And then, when that had not succeeded, he had invited Sir Wilhelm and Mr. Brockfield to Kent knowing that they would thoroughly overwhelm Peter with their presence.

And yet, through the long, restless night it was not Barth's outrageous behavior that had haunted her but the memory of his husky words.

It has never been my intention to be unfaithful to my wife.

He sounded so sincere, as if he truly cared that she believe his vow. And the way he had gazed deep in her eyes had stolen her very breath.

Was her grandfather right? Had she allowed her wounded pride at being abandoned in Kent while he enjoyed the pleasures of London to sway her judgment? Had she been too harsh? Too unforgiving?

Isa, what a fool you are, she chastised herself.

What did she care if Barth vowed to become a virtual saint once he wed? She had already decided she was not to be his bride.

Had she not?

Gazing out the window, Isa felt a shiver race through her body. She wished that Barth had not returned to Kent. With him far away, it had been easy to convince herself that her feelings for him had been childish fantasies and that she had matured enough to recognize substance from charm.

But since his return . . .

Botheration.

She did not want to admit that her heart still halted the moment he walked into the room or that the day seemed a bit dull until she knew that she would be in his company.

No, she was worse than a fool, she assured herself. She was clearly noddy.

Lost in her brooding thoughts, Isa had nearly forgotten her mother, seated in a far chair, stitching on a sampler, until her voice echoed through the vast salon.

"Really, Isa, is something the matter?"

She instinctively stiffened at the accusation. She had no intention of confessing her troubled thoughts to her mother. Louise Lawford would have her halfway to the altar before she knew what was occurring.

"Of course not."

"You have been peering out the window all morning." Mrs. Lawford favored her daughter with a coy smile. "Are you expecting a visitor?"

Of course she was, she granted with a pang of disgust. She waited every day for the sight of Lord Wickton.

"I am merely admiring the fine weather," she answered, forcing herself to lie. "I believe the lilacs are coming into bloom."

Her mother refused to be put off. "I thought perhaps you were awaiting Lord Wickton."

Isa battled the betraying blush. "Why should you suppose any such thing?"

"Why should I not?" Louise smiled in a decidedly smug manner. "He has called every day since your illness."

"I am well now," Isa pointed out, uncertain whom she was attempting to convince. "Besides, he is entertaining guests."

The older woman merely laughed. "Silly goose. I witnessed Lord Wickton's conduct last evening. He could not stray from your side. Mark my words, he will be calling."

Isa regarded her mother with a faint frown.

"I hope that you are not still harboring the belief that I will wed Lord Wickton."

"But of course," Louise retorted. "Even you must admit that he has proven to be all that is proper in a gentleman since his return to Kent."

"He could hardly be otherwise in such a rural community."

Her mother gave a disapproving sniff at her stubborn expression.

"And what of his devotion during your illness?" she demanded. "I must tell you that it warmed my heart to witness him tend to your slightest need. What other gentleman would have been so thoughtful?"

Isa caught her breath. The truth was that no one could have been more patient or more caring. He had known precisely how to ease her discomfort and bring a smile to her face.

"He was very kind," she murmured.

"Far more kind than the vicar's son."

Isa swallowed a weary sigh, turning back toward the window.

"Please, Mother."

"What? I am speaking no less than the truth. You could find no better husband than Lord Wickton."

"I . . ." Isa's protest was cut short as she glimpsed the slender form of Peter Effinton scurrying across the courtyard. Her eyes widened at the uncharacteristic haste. As a rule, Peter shuffled through the countryside, barely aware of his surroundings. She could only wonder at his odd haste.

"What is it?" her mother demanded.

"It is Peter, and he appears to be in an uncommon hurry."

"Fah. Ridiculous boy."

Isa turned back with a warning frown. "Please be polite, Mother."

Mrs. Lawford merely shifted so that her back was toward the door. It was obvious she had no intention of even greeting their unexpected guest. With a grimace, Isa moved across the room. Did everything have to be so complicated?

Within moments, the butler was pulling open the door with a slight bow.

"Mr. Effinton is here to see you."

"Please show him in, Rushton."

"Very good."

The servant disappeared, only to be swiftly replaced by a flushed Peter. Isa blinked in mild surprise as she noted his disarrayed hair and rumpled shirt.

"Good morning, Peter. This is an unexpected pleasure."

"Yes, well, I suppose it is frightfully early for a call, but I simply had to speak with you."

She raised her brows, her curiosity thoroughly roused. "Has something occurred?"

"Yes, I should say so."

Wondering what could possibly have roused the placid scholar to such enthusiasm, Isa waved a hand toward the window seat.

"Why do we not make ourselves comfortable?" Moving to the seat, Isa settled herself on the cushion; then, waiting for Peter to join her, she offered him an encouraging smile. "Now, what has happened?"

Quite astonishingly, Peter reached out to grasp her hands in a strong grip.

"You will never guess who called on me this morning."

She gave a soft laugh. From Peter's tone it might have been the prince regent himself.

"I fear I haven't the faintest notion."

"Mr. Brockfield," he pronounced in awed tones.

"How wonderful," Isa congratulated with genuine pleasure. "You must have impressed him last evening."

His thin face flushed with excitement. "That is precisely what he said. Can you imagine?"

"I am not at all surprised."

His grip on her hands tightened to a near-painful level. "Not only that, but Isa, he has offered me a post."

Isa forgot her crushed fingers as her smile slowly faded. "What?"

"He wishes me to be his secretary," Peter elaborated, oblivious as always to Isa's reaction. "To assist him in his studies and even his lectures."

A cold, hard ball settled in the pit of her stomach.

"He wishes you to leave Kent?"

"Well, of course I will travel with him," Peter retorted, as if surprised she would even ask such an obvious question. "He said that we shall be leaving for Brussels within the month. Is that not the most glorious news?"

Glorious was not the word Isa would have used. She pulled her hands free as she allowed her budding suspicion to flower.

She did not believe for a moment that Mr. Brockfield had been so taken with Peter that he had rushed to the vicarage this morning to offer him a position. No matter how brilliant Peter might be, a gentleman such as Mr. Brockfield could have his choice of willing scholars throughout England. Why would he travel to the midst of the country and suddenly conclude he was in dire need of a secretary?

No, this had the Machiavellian hand of Lord Wickton written all over it.

A sharp, nearly unbearable pain lanced through

her heart. Would Barth go to such lengths? After all, it was one thing to dangle temptations or offer distractions, but to actually intrude into an innocent man's life, to manipulate his very future.

Was anyone that arrogant?

"Isa."

With a blink, Isa realized that Peter was regarding her with a gathering frown.

"Yes?" she murmured, attempting to gather her scattered thoughts.

"Is something the matter?"

She could hardly confess the truth. Still, she felt the need to offer some hint of warning.

"This is all rather sudden, is it not?" she cautiously pointed out. "You did just meet last evening. He knows little about you."

Peter happily shrugged. "He remembers a paper he read of mine at Oxford. He said that it had convinced him I was worthy of such an extraordinary opportunity."

"How very convenient."

"I cannot believe my good fortune."

"Yes, it is remarkably unbelievable," she muttered. "What do you suppose is the likelihood of Mr. Brockfield arriving in Kent and meeting you precisely when he is in need of a secretary?"

"I must thank God for my blessings."

Isa gave a sharp, humorless laugh. "I believe there is someone nearer at hand you can thank."

Peter gave a bemused blink. "What?"

Isa bit back her impetuous words. Whatever the reason for Mr. Brockfield's offer, it truly was an extraordinary opportunity for Peter. She could not steal his moment of glory.

"Nothing."

"Well, I must go." Peter surged to his feet, his eyes glowing with anticipation. "I merely wished to share such wondrous news."

Hardly an emotional farewell, she wryly acknowledged. Not that she expected anything more. Still, she hoped he would find happiness.

"Peter," she called softly.

"Yes."

"Good luck."

"Thank you." With a distracted bow, he turned to hurry out the door.

Drawing in a deep breath, Isa slowly rose to her feet. While she might wish Peter well, she did not wish Barth such luck.

Indeed, she very much wished to have his handsome head upon a platter.

"This time, Lord Wickton, you have gone beyond the pale . . . ," she muttered.

Having spoken with Andrew and been assured that Peter Effinton would soon be safely on his way to London, Barth settled Sir Wilhelm with his grandmother and made his way back to the main wing.

He was feeling decidedly pleased with himself.

It was just as he had predicted from the outset. A well-laid plan, the proper weapons, and success was assured.

Soon Peter would be away from Kent, and Isa

would have to admit that her absurd attachment to the young gentleman had been a mere figment of her imagination. From there it was only a matter of convincing her that he himself was a far more dependable prospect as a husband.

Strolling into the library, Barth was sifting through the morning mail when the door was thrust open and the butler stepped into the room.

"My lord," the servant murmured with a faint bow.

"Yes?"

"Miss Lawford is here," Gatson announced in disapproving tones. "She says that she wishes to speak with you . . . alone."

Barth raised his brows in surprise. Isa had not deliberately sought his company since his return to Kent. And to do so in such an unconventional manner was decidedly unlike her.

He tossed aside the large stack of letters. "Send her in."

The butler gave a stiff bow. "Very good, my lord."

Smoothing the jade coat he had matched with a pale yellow waistcoat and buff breeches, Barth waited with a flare of anticipation for his unexpected guest. He had resigned himself to not seeing her until later in the day. He was glad she had taken matters into her own hands.

When the door opened, Barth felt his blood quicken at the sight of her slender frame, clothed in a simple gown of mist blue. Without thought, he was moving forward to lift her hand for a lingering kiss.

"Ah, Isa, what a delightful surprise."

"Is it?" she demanded, determinedly pulling her hand from his grasp.

Lifting his head, he studied her set features and smoldering amber eyes. It did not appear as if she had come this morning to confess a change of heart.

"Is something amiss, Isa?"

"Surely you knew that I would come when I discovered the truth," she demanded with a familiar tilt of her chin. "Or did you think me too stupid to see through your obvious interference?"

His gaze narrowed at her accusing tone. "I fear that I am not following your meaning. What interference have I supposedly performed?"

"You know quite well you invited Mr. Brockfield here for the sole purpose of having him offer Peter a post as his secretary."

Barth stiffened. Good lord, Peter must have rushed to her doorstep at the crack of dawn. Still, they might as well settle the matter of Effinton sooner rather than later.

He crossed his arms over the width of his chest. "As a matter of fact, I only invited Sir Wilhelm and Mr. Brockfield to prove to you that Peter's true love would always be his studies. The notion of having Andrew offer him a position only came when I realized they were so obviously suited to one another."

Her eyes widened at his smooth explanation. "So you admit it."

"Why should I not?"

"You are . . . despicable."

"Why?" A gathering frown marred his wide brow. "Because I am determined to marry you?"

She was clearly unimpressed by his motives.

"Because you haven't the least concern for anyone besides yourself. Did it ever occur to you that you had no right to interfere in Peter's life?"

"Interfere?" Barth felt a rising sense of irritation. Really, she was being thoroughly unreasonable. "I provided an opportunity that he would never have achieved on his own. Do you believe Peter would prefer to remain living with his father in Kent when he could be traveling throughout Europe with Mr. Brockfield?"

"That is not the point," she gritted.

"Is it not?"

"No."

"Then what is?"

Her hands slapped onto her hips. "The point is that you decided Peter was an obstacle to what you wanted, and like any obstacle, you simply swept him aside. You did not even consider that he is a fellow human being."

Dash it all. She made him sound as if he were some ogre.

"If I did not care, he would have simply disappeared in the local river," he pointed out.

Her lips thinned. "That is not amusing."

"Well, it is certainly not the heavy-handed tragedy you are making it. Andrew is satisfied, and your Mr. Effinton is delighted. What is the harm?"

Her eyes rolled heavenward as if his stupidity surpassed all bearing.

"And what of me?"

His frown deepened. By gads, how was he to know what he was being accused of if she did not explain?

"What of you?"

"Obviously you have no concern for Peter, but you claimed to be my friend."

"I am."

"And so you lie, deceive, and manipulate to take away a gentleman you know that I care about?"

Barth ground his teeth. Did she purposely view him in the worst possible light? Anyone would think he had kidnapped Peter Effinton and shipped him to the colonies, if not tortured and buried him in the dungeon.

"I wanted to avert you from making a terrible mistake. Effinton could never make you happy."

Far from appeased, Isa gave a humorless laugh.

"You must think me a witless fool. You did not care if I would be happy with Peter or even if it would break my heart if he was taken away. You had decided that I was to be your countess, and nothing was going to stand in your path. Certainly nothing so insignificant as my feelings."

Barth stilled as a flare of pain twisted through his gut.

"Is your heart broken?"

An unreadable mask settled onto her tiny countenance. "Does it matter?"

He stepped forward, battling the urge to pull her into his arms and effectively prove that Effinton meant nothing to her. He would wager his last quid she never responded to that milksop as she did to him.

"You have not answered my question."

"And I do not intend to," she informed him stiffly.

Barth's hands clenched at his sides. "He does not deserve you."

Her gaze narrowed. "And you do?"

"I shall do my best."

"Oh, no." She gave a slow shake of her head. "You will not be given the opportunity." Something that might have been pain flared through her magnificent eyes. "Good-bye, my lord. Please do not attempt to see me again."

Momentarily shocked by the bleak demand, Barth watched in silence as Isa turned and fled the room.

What the devil had just happened?

Isa was supposed to be furious with Peter. After all, he was the one abandoning her without regard to her feelings, while he was remaining to offer her marriage.

But instead . . .

Abruptly realizing that Isa was slipping away, Barth hurried into the hall. But it was too late. There was no sign of the woman who had so disrupted his morning.

Blast . . .

Fourteen

Feeling decidedly abused, Barth stormed through the hall to his grandmother's wing. He paid scant heed to the servants who dodged out of his furious path.

Women.

They should all be . . .

Well, he was not quite certain what should be done with them beyond keeping them far away from him.

He had done everything in his power to win Isa's hand in marriage. More than he would have done for any other woman, he seethed with a sense of injustice. And yet she had been determined to condemn him as an unfeeling monster from the moment he had returned to Kent.

For God's sake, he might as well have remained in London.

Reaching his grandmother's private salon, Barth entered without bothering to announce himself. With an unconsciously dramatic motion, he closed the door and marched to the center of the room.

"That is it."

Seated in her favorite chair, Lady Sarah laid aside her cup of tea and regarded him with a faint smile.

"Goodness. Now what has occurred?"

"I am finished with all females."

Predictably, the older woman merely laughed at his ominous threat.

"I presume you are referring to Isa?"

"Why must she be so bloody stubborn?" he growled.

"Is your grand battle plan not a success, then?"

Success? More like a ghastly failure.

"I have done everything to woo her as a proper suitor." He paced across the carpet with a restless motion. "I flattered her, I seduced her, and I even cared for her when she was ill. Still she prefers that namby-pamby who barely notices she is about."

"I thought that you intended to rid her of Mr. Effinton's company?"

He smiled wryly as he recalled his naive boast. Until this morning, he had never considered the possibility that his determination to win the battle might lose him the war.

"I did."

Lady Sarah raised her silver brows. "And?"

He abruptly turned to face his grandmother with a grim expression.

"And now Isa never wishes to clap eyes upon me again."

Lady Sarah appeared far from surprised by his pronouncement. Indeed, she regarded him with a faint hint of sympathy.

"Really, Barth, what did you expect?"

He frowned at her absurd question. "Certainly not this."

She gave a click of her tongue as she leaned forward and stabbed him with a piercing regard.

"For a gentleman who is a reputed rake, you know very little about women."

His nose flared at the insult. Although he was certainly no rake, he could boast a measure of success with the fairer sex. Wasn't that what had supposedly landed him in this beastly brew in the first place?

Of course, he readily admitted that he hadn't the faintest clue to comprehending Isa Lawford. She was without a doubt the most troublesome maiden it had ever been his misfortune to encounter.

"I presume you intend to explain that remark?" he demanded of his grandmother.

"Isa is not a bounty of war to be won by the better general," Lady Sarah readily retorted. "She is a woman with feelings."

That strange, decidedly unpleasant pang once again twisted his heart.

"Yes, feelings for Peter Effinton."

"*Fah.*" His grandmother snorted.

"What?"

"She does not love Peter Effinton."

He threw up his hands in exasperation. His grandmother was right. He knew nothing of the devious workings of the female mind.

"Then why is she so furious?"

"Because she is afraid."

Barth abruptly halted his pacing. "Of me?"

"Of her feelings for you," Lady Sarah clarified.

"She loved you once and was hurt. She can have no desire to risk such betrayal again."

Could it be true? he inwardly wondered. Could Isa's continued resistance to his charm simply be a feminine fear of being hurt?

It was certainly a thought more preferable to the belief that she desired another.

Still, that did not solve his current difficulties.

"I have promised I will care for her," he informed his grandmother. "What more can I do?"

Lady Sarah appeared thoroughly unimpressed by his confession.

"You claim to care for her, and yet you plotted to have her only friend removed from Kent."

Bloody hell, she sounded just like Isa, Barth seethed.

"Would you prefer that I had hired him so that he and Isa could wed and live in their pretty little cottage?"

"Yes."

Barth was stunned at the simple answer. Had his grandmother grown a bit daft? Or was she just being difficult?

"What?"

Lady Sarah smiled, clearly reading his less than flattering thoughts.

"That is what someone who cared for her would do."

Allow Isa to wed another? Never.

"She belongs to me."

His grandmother studied his harsh expression for

a long moment; then, with a small sigh, she settled back into her cushions.

"Did you know, Barth, that your grandfather was engaged to another when we first met?"

Barth bit back his instinctive response. For once he was in no humor for his grandmother's rambling tales of the past. He wanted Isa. And he had somehow thought Lady Sarah would possess the necessary insight to reveal how he could convince her that she was making a ghastly mistake.

Still, he respected his grandmother far too much to reveal his annoyance. Instead, he gave a vague shrug.

"No."

Lady Sarah chose to ignore his obvious lack of enthusiasm as a reminiscent smile touched her aged countenance.

"Miss Fellwan," she continued. "A lovely girl with the most charming stutter."

"Grandmother . . ."

"Of course, the moment I met the dashing Lord Wickton, I tumbled madly in love," she said, overriding his attempts to steer the conversation back to Isa. "And despite his best efforts, I could tell he returned my feelings."

Barth was barely paying heed to the low words. "How fortunate."

"Actually, it was most unfortunate," the older woman argued. "Whatever our attachment, he was promised to another."

"Obviously he ended the promise."

Lady Sarah gave a slow shake of her head. "No, he

did not. Despite our feelings, he refused to betray Miss Fellwan."

Barth gave a short, disbelieving laugh. "Good God, Grandmother, please do not confess that the two of you never wed."

She wagged a heavily jeweled finger in his direction. "Of course we did. But not until Miss Fellwan had decided that she preferred to wed Lord Lanfield."

It was a very nice story, but Barth gave an impatient sigh. Really, he did not have time for such nonsense.

"What does this have to do with Isa?" he demanded.

"Can you not see, Barth?" Lady Sarah regarded him as if he were being deliberately stupid—not a sensation that he particularly enjoyed. "It was the very fact that your grandfather refused to hurt Miss Fellwan that convinced me that I could always trust him with my heart. If he had simply tossed his fiancée aside, how could I not fear that he would someday treat me in a similar manner?"

Barth grappled to follow his grandmother's meaning. Not an easy task for a gentleman who believed in fighting for what he desired. To simply stand aside seemed tantamount to conceding defeat.

"And you would have preferred to lose him forever?"

Lady Sarah's gaze never wavered. "Yes."

Barth gave an impatient growl. It was easy to make such noble claims now. He could not imagine that the two were so resigned to their fate at the time.

"I am not my grandfather," he charged with a relentless expression.

A sudden tenderness softened his grandmother's features. "No, but you do possess a good heart. If you truly care for Isa, then you will place her happiness before your own."

He had not changed.

Pacing through the salon, Isa pressed a hand to her aching heart. After all the assurances that he cared for her and even the long days he had comforted her during her illness, he was still the same arrogant beast that she had branded him.

What else but arrogance would allow a gentleman to behave in such a manner?

He had not cared if Peter would be happy with his new position or even if he wished to leave Kent. He had simply desired to send the potential suitor far away from her.

He had not even considered her own feelings. After all, he did not realize she had accepted the fact that her attachment for Peter was not love. As far as he was concerned, she still desired to be Peter's wife. And yet he had used every means at his considerable disposal to keep them apart.

He was still the same Lord Wickton.

So why, then, did she feel like weeping?

Because despite all of her sensible determination to keep him at arms' length, and all her proud claims that she had thrust him out of her heart, she still loved him.

She choked back a sob of despair. Heaven above, how could she be so weak?

She had always known that Barth would never return her love. To him she was simply the woman that he was expected to wed.

And that was why she had been so furious with his cavalier treatment of poor Peter. Barth might not love her, but in his mind she was Wickton property. And no one poached upon Wickton property. He did not allow his possessions to be stolen by another.

She should never have agreed to see him after his return to Kent, she told herself sternly. In her prideful manner she had convinced herself that she was impervious to his charm. After all, she had already suffered and recovered from the pangs of first love. In truth, however, she had never stopped loving him.

Or at least she loved the man who had taught her to swim and brought her flowers when she was ill and kissed her in the garden.

As for the rest . . .

Well, he would never change. He would always be arrogant. He would always place his own needs first. And he would never love her.

She was a fool to hope for a moment it could be otherwise.

"Please, my lord, Miss Lawford does not wish to be disturbed."

The sound of Rushton's voice echoed through the open door, making Isa stiffen with alarm. No. Surely not even Barth would be so bold as to follow her after their unpleasant encounter this morning.

But there was no mistaking Lord Wickton's stern tone. "I must see her."

"My lord, I must insist that you leave."

"I will stay here all day if need be."

"Lord Wickton . . ."

Without even realizing that she was moving, Isa was across the room and standing in the doorway to regard the anxious servant and the towering lord. A pang twisted her heart at the sight of the lean features and well-molded frame, but none of her inner weakness was allowed to be revealed on her stern countenance.

"For goodness' sake, let him in, Rushton," she called.

At the sound of her voice, Barth instantly thrust his way past the disapproving servant.

"Isa."

With a stiff back, she returned to the center of the salon. She waited until she heard the sound of the door closing; then, willing herself to maintain her composure, she turned around to face the gentleman who had once again disrupted her life.

"What is it that you wanted, my lord?"

He stepped toward her, his gaze closely studying her pale features.

"I have come to speak with you."

"Once again ignoring my own desires in the matter," she pointed out.

Something that might have been annoyance flashed over his face before he had swiftly dampened the emotion.

"I want to apologize."

"Do you?"

"Yes."

"For what?" she demanded in cold tones.

"For interfering in Mr. Effinton's life. As you said, I had no right."

The words were said with a smooth ease, but Isa was not swayed for a moment. He was not sorry for his actions, merely that they had not succeeded.

"Fine." She gave a faint nod of her head. "You have apologized. Now you can leave."

He frowned. "Did you hear me?"

"Yes."

"I have admitted that I was wrong."

Her lips twisted. She wondered what it cost his pride to make such an admission.

"And that is supposed to make everything all right?"

The hazel eyes flashed. "What more do you want from me?"

Your love. The betraying words flashed through her mind before she angrily thrust them aside.

She would no longer hope for what never could be hers.

"Tell me, Barth, why are you so determined to marry me?"

"I have told you." He carefully watched her reaction, as if determining how best to convince her of his sincerity. "I think we should suit very well."

"You did not think so when you fled five years ago," she reminded him in dry tones.

"I was young, and I resented the thought of having

my future determined for me. Is that so difficult to understand?"

"No, but I do not believe that it is because you have suddenly realized that we are suited that you have changed your mind."

"What do you mean?" he demanded.

Her chin tilted. "You could not bear the thought of losing to another gentleman."

An unexpected hint of color stained his cheeks. "Absurd."

"Is it? You had no interest in me beyond my dowry until you realized I might love another."

His mouth opened as if to deny the accusation; then, meeting the glitter in her amber eyes, he gave a reluctant shrug.

"I will admit that I was angered by your interest in Mr. Effinton."

"You saw me as your possession, and you were determined no one else would have me."

His hands clenched at his sides. He was clearly unaccustomed to having his will countered.

"I have done everything possible to prove I will make you a good husband."

"No, you have done everything possible to take me from Peter." She gave a shake of her head. "It is just like that ghost story you are so fond of telling me—about the knight and his stolen bride. Perhaps if that knight had not been so intent on revenge, he would not have killed his bride."

He stilled, his expression becoming grim. "And you believe that I care more about revenge than you? You think I am that shallow?"

A darkness entered the hazel eyes, and for an absurd moment Isa dared to believe that more than his pride was wounded at her determined resistance. Then, with a silent chastisement of her susceptible heart, she determinedly turned and blindly gazed out the window.

"Yes," she murmured.

He heaved an exasperated sigh. "So what do you want from me?"

It took a pained moment before she could force the words through her dry throat.

"I told you earlier."

"You never wish to see me again?" he demanded in disbelief.

"Precisely."

She heard him scrape in a sharp breath. "And what will you do?"

"Do?"

"Do you intend to wed Peter Effinton?"

She gave an unsteady laugh. "That is hardly possible now."

He was silent for so long that Isa began to wonder if he had simply walked out on her. Then, just as she prepared to turn about, she heard his soft words.

"No, I suppose not."

She closed her eyes as a pain ripped through her body. How desperately she desired to admit that it did not matter why he wished her to be his bride, that she only longed to be at his side. It was only the bleak image of belonging to him and yet never being a part of his life that kept her determination intact.

"I believe that we have said everything that there is to say."

"Yes. Indeed, I shall make it easy for you."

That did have her turning back, and with a sense of shock, she discovered that he appeared as wounded as she felt.

Odd considering his own heart was not being torn in two.

"What do you mean?"

"I am returning to London," he pronounced in grim tones.

Unbelievably, her pain managed to deepen.

"Of course," she said through white lips. "You must find a bride."

His features twisted with a stark anger. "I assure you I have lost all interest in brides." He gave a stiff bow. "Good-bye, Isa."

Caught off guard by the bitterness in his tone, Isa watched in silence as he stalked from the room.

Then, pressing a hand to her trembling lips, she sank onto the window seat.

"Good-bye . . . my love," she whispered.

Fifteen

Staggering down the street in a decidedly inebriated state, Barth attempted to keep his head from spinning.

London was precisely as he remembered.

Within hours of returning to his town house, he had been flooded with invitations to routs, balls, and every social event imaginable. He had also received several suggestive notes from the lovely Monique, who had swiftly discovered his return. But while Barth forced himself to spend his evenings with the elegant ton and devoted the late evenings to the various gaming halls, he felt nothing beyond an aching wish to be back in Kent.

It was ludicrous. He should be delighted at being back among civilized society. This was how he had once thought he wished to devote the rest of his life. Yet night after night he had to force himself to enter his waiting carriage, and night after night he drank himself into a stupor in the hopes it would end the aching dreams of Isa.

Of course, it was a wasted effort. There was not a

moment that he did not search his surroundings for a futile sight of her golden hair or a night he did not wake with tortured dreams of holding her in his arms.

Not even the knowledge that he should be searching for an heiress could penetrate his dark mood. He was done with duty. If he could not have Isa, he would not have any bride.

"The devil take all women . . . ," he muttered as he shoved past the servant who was attempting to block his way into his favorite club.

He needed a place to rest before hailing a cab and being returned home. He had long since dismissed his own carriage with the assurance that he intended to gamble away the night.

Ignoring the insistent entreaties from the servant that he halt a moment, Barth weaved his way up the steps and into a large room. It was not until an older, far more commanding servant stepped into his path that he came to an abrupt halt.

"My lord, perhaps you should come with me. I have some fresh coffee in the back."

Barth frowned in an ominous manner. By gads, all he wished was a place to sit and a large decanter of brandy.

"Stand aside, Huber," he commanded in loud tones.

The servant held up his hands in a pleading motion. "My lord, please."

Barth swayed unsteadily. "Stand aside or be prepared to defend yourself."

Intent on the servant, Barth was taken off guard

as a large, raven-haired gentleman abruptly put his arm about his shoulders.

"Wickton, come along," Lord Brasleigh commanded.

Thoroughly startled to be confronted by his friend, Barth allowed himself to be led across the room, not even protesting as Lord Challmond stepped forward and pressed him into the wing chair.

"Challmond? Brasleigh?" He blinked in muddled surprise. "What the devil are you doing here?"

"Clearly the same thing you have been doing for quite some time," Simon retorted in dry tones.

Barth turned toward him, his fuzzy gaze landing on the decanter beside the chair.

"Ah . . . brandy. Just what I need."

"Coffee," Philip corrected as he whisked the spirits out of reach and handed it to the hovering Huber. "Now, why are you not in Kent with your new bride?"

An unnaturally bitter expression twisted Barth's countenance.

"There is no bride."

Simon regarded his friend in surprise. "I thought the marriage was arranged?"

"As did I." Barth's head flopped onto the soft leather, his lids fluttering shut in weary pain. "Unfortunately, the bride has decided that she prefers another. And I must say I do not blame her. He is an absolutely brilliant gentleman without a fault to be discovered. And believe me, I have tried."

He missed the knowing glance between his friends.

"That is rather a bad break, but she is not the only

maiden in England. You will soon find another bride," Philip drawled.

Barth slowly raised his gaze, not surprised when the two gentlemen winced at his darkened eyes and pain-lined countenance. He was well aware that he appeared like those poor wounded soldiers who knew beyond a doubt they were not making it home.

"Yes, there are no doubt any number of maidens willing to become the countess of Wickton." He grimaced. "A pity I do not bloody well want them."

Philip gave another humorless laugh. "Well, are we not a sad trio? What happened to the 'Casanova Club'? Love them and leave them wishing for more?"

"It is all that Gypsy's fault," Barth muttered. "She and her devil's curse."

"Absurd." Simon gave a shake of his head.

Barth stabbed him with a jaundiced glare. "Then you have not tumbled into the stormy seas of love?"

"Love?" Simon grimaced.

"My lord."

With a startled blink, Simon turned to discover a servant hovering at his side with an anxious expression.

"Yes?"

"A message has been delivered for you."

"Thank you." Simon accepted the sealed note and broke it open with a faint frown.

Scanning the neatly scrawled message, Simon abruptly crumpled it into a ball and tossed it into the fire.

"Damnation."

"Troubles?" Philip demanded in concern.

"It is from Locky."

"Locky?" Barth hiccuped. He recalled the solid, utterly dependable gentleman with a sense of pleasure. He had always enjoyed Locky's company. "Where the devil is he?"

"Devonshire." Simon clenched his fists. "I have to leave."

"Wait." Philip placed a hand on his shoulder, his expression somber. "Is there something that we can do to help?"

Simon met the silver gaze with a determined smile. "As a matter of fact, you can wish me luck," he said as he came to a sudden decision. "I am off to win the heart of the woman I love."

Barth watched his friend's determined retreat with a dark frown.

"The woman he loves?" he slurred, grimacing at the now-familiar stab of pain. Surely he could not be jealous of Simon? "Poor sod. Where is that brandy?"

"I believe you have indulged enough for one evening." Philip regarded him in a searching manner as he slowly returned to his seat.

Barth gave a bitter laugh. "I have not indulged nearly enough."

Philip frowned. "What troubles you?"

"Isa Lawford troubles me," Barth muttered.

"I thought you did not wish to wed the chit?"

He briefly recalled his selfish regrets at being forced down the aisle and his arrogant confidence that Isa was desperate to become his countess.

"I was a bloody fool."

"Then you wish her to be your wife?"

Barth did not hesitate. "Yes."

The silver eyes seemed to bore straight to his very heart.

"Do you love her?"

"Love?" Barth closed his weary eyes. "What is that?"

"How do you feel when you are near her?"

"As if my guts are being twisted into a knot," he retorted with brutal honesty. "Is that love?"

"I certainly hope not," Philip retorted in a shockingly harsh voice.

Barth was too enwrapped in his own misery to take notice of his friend's peculiar manner, and slowly opening his eyes, he banged a fist on the arm of his chair.

"But the beastly thing is that I can not get her out of my mind," he gritted in anger. "I came to London to enjoy my freedom. After all, I have spent a lifetime being smothered by the knowledge I would have to wed Isa Lawford to save the Wickton family from disgrace. I should be relieved at the thought she has refused to become my wife."

"But you are not relieved?" Philip demanded.

Barth shuddered at the long days and even longer nights he had endured since his return to London.

"I have never been so bloody miserable in all my life," he confessed. "Isa may no longer be my fiancée, but she refuses to leave me in peace."

"Do not tell me," Philip commanded, his elegant features twisting with an inner pain. "She is there every time you close your eyes. You smell her scent in the air, and when you awake in the morning, your arms ache because she is not lying beside you."

Barth suddenly leaned forward, his expression one of disbelief.

"How did you know?" he demanded.

Philip's features abruptly settled into their more familiar sardonic lines as he shrugged aside the question.

"What will you do?"

Barth clenched his hands. "Nothing."

"Nothing?"

"I have been informed that a true gentleman should bow out with as much grace as possible."

Philip narrowed his silver gaze. "I have never known you to give up, Wickton. Remember when we were surrounded by those damned Frenchies and our commander wanted to retreat? You pulled out your sword and demanded that we fight our way through."

Of course Barth remembered. He had been so arrogantly confident that he could best any foe. It had taken a golden-haired maiden to prove he was vulnerable.

"I would rather face a regiment of Frenchies than a devious woman. At least I knew what was expected of me."

Philip offered a sharp laugh. "Here. Here."

Barth shook his head at his own stupidity. "You were wise not to become entangled in the dangerous lures of a female."

"Yes, I am all that is wise," Philip retorted in mocking tones. "What will you do?"

It was a question that Barth had refused to consider. Even with the knowledge that he was in debt and that Graystone would soon tumble into disrepair, he could not summon the energy to care.

"I do not know."

"What do you want?"

Want? He wanted Isa as his wife. He wanted her in his arms, where she belonged. He wanted her to fill his nursery with children.

He wanted . . . he wanted . . . he wanted . . .

Bloody hell. He sounded as selfish and self-absorbed as Isa had branded him.

Lord, what had he done?

The sudden vision of her as he had last seen her rose to mind—her tiny face white with loss and her haunted amber eyes. A knifing pain ripped through his heart.

With all his determination to win, he had never thought what he was doing to Isa. He had convinced himself that it was for her own good, that he would make her a far better husband than Peter Effinton. But now, recalling that heartrending expression of loss on her face, he abruptly realized he had never truly thought of her at all.

It was just as his grandmother had accused.

It had only been his own needs that he had considered.

He had been a thorough blackguard.

"Barth?"

With a blink, Barth realized that his companion was regarding him with mounting concern.

"What do I want?" Barth rasped. "I want to see Isa smile."

A thick silence fell as the two men regarded each other for a long moment, then Philip slowly gave a nod of his head.

"Yes."

"Bloody hell."

With an unsteady motion, Barth rose to his feet. Despite the brandy still muddling his thoughts, he was sharply conscious of what he had to do.

Regardless of the cost to himself.

Philip also rose, laying a hand on his shoulder.

"Where are you going?"

Barth gave a short laugh. "To do the one good thing I may ever do in my miserable, self-indulgent life."

Unaware she was being closely watched, Isa pushed the piece of egg from one side of her plate to the other. She then absently offered the slice of ham the same treatment. It was not that she particularly enjoyed toying with her food, but it was certainly preferable to attempting to eat the now-cold breakfast.

It had been the same every morning since Barth had announced that he was leaving for London. No matter how sternly she chided herself for behaving as a nitwit and assured herself she would never go into a romantic decline over any mere man, the truth was that she found it difficult to make herself rise every morning.

Her only hope was that this current distemper

would eventually pass. After all, with Barth in London, she would not have to fear seeing him about the neighborhood. In time her pain would ease, and she would consider her future without the bleakness it currently held.

Her mother interrupted her dark musings with impatient tones. "Isa, you must eat something."

Reluctantly, Isa lifted her head and met her mother's worried gaze.

"I am not hungry, Mother."

Louise gave a click of her tongue. "Well, I do not like to say this, my dear, but you are beginning to look positively haggard."

Isa did not need her mother's less-than-flattering statement to assure her that she was appearing far too pale and thin.

"Thank you."

"I am only saying this for your own good. I should not like to see your beauty fade at such an early age."

Isa's lips twisted with a wry amusement. "You mean, before I can capture a husband."

Her mother allowed a martyred expression to settle on her long face.

"Well, for that . . . I have quite given up hope that you will ever behave in a reasonable manner."

"I know you too well, Mother." Isa pushed aside her plate. "You will never give up hope of unloading me onto some unsuspecting nobleman."

"Isa," Louise protested at her blunt accusation.

Isa wrinkled her nose in regret. It was grossly unfair to take her ill humor out on her mother.

"Forgive me." She slowly rose to her feet. "I believe I shall take a stroll in the garden."

Only marginally mollified, Louise gave a faint sniff. "Stay out of the sun. Becoming freckled will hardly improve your appearance."

"Very well, Mother." Isa forced herself to maintain her annoyance. Leaving the breakfast room, Isa moved down the hall and into a small alcove that opened into the garden. Promptly forgetting her mother's warning, she strolled past the garden and toward the lake. She simply wished to be away from the house and the well-intentioned but meddlesome company of her mother.

Perhaps she should consider visiting her great-aunt in York, she told herself with a sigh. A change of scenery just might take her mind off her troubled thoughts. If nothing else, it would remove her from her mother's desperate search for another suitable son-in-law.

Bending down to pluck a blooming wildflower, Isa was unaware of the approaching rider. It was not until the sound of footsteps penetrated her muddled thoughts that she sharply glanced up to discover the tall, chestnut-haired gentleman standing mere feet away.

For a crazed moment, Isa thought she might actually swoon. Barth could not be here. He was in London searching for a wealthy bride. But there was no imagining his solid frame and the chiseled beauty of his countenance.

She pressed a hand to her racing heart. "Barth."

He performed a slight bow, his oddly fevered gaze never leaving her pale face.

"Good morning, Isa."

"What . . ." Her voice broke, and she forced herself to take a steadying breath. Dear lord, he was so magnificent, she acknowledged with a pang of loss. And she had missed him so desperately. "I did not realize you had returned to Graystone."

"I returned only an hour ago."

That explained why her mother was not leaping for joy.

"I see."

He searched her overly thin features and the unmistakable shadows beneath her eyes.

"How are you?"

"Quite well," she lied. She could hardly confess she was withering with unrequited love.

Predictably, he was not fooled for a moment. "You look pale. And you've lost weight."

A hint of annoyance stirred through her clinging lethargy. What right did he have to judge her appearance when he was entirely to blame?

"I have told you I am well. What are you doing here?"

"I have brought you something."

"What?"

With oddly jerky movements, Barth pressed a thick packet into her hand. She was so startled by the unexpected motion, she did not even glance through the papers.

"What is this?"

"I have set up an allowance from my estate to go to Mr. Effinton."

An allowance for Peter? It made no sense.

"I do not understand."

"It will give Mr. Effinton a yearly income so that he will be able to set up his own establishment and continue his studies." His voice was expressionless, but Isa did not miss the tension in his jaw or the manner in which his hands clenched and unclenched. "It is not much, but with a thrifty wife, he will no doubt scrape by."

She slowly shook her head, feeling uncommonly dim-witted.

"But why? Why would you do this?"

For a moment, she thought he would refuse to answer; then, turning to gaze over the lake, he gave a restless shrug.

"When I went to London, I was determined to forget you." He gave a short laugh. "Indeed, I wanted nothing more than to forget you even existed."

Her heart twisted. "And did you?"

"No. It did not matter how many parties I attended or how many bottles of brandy I consumed, you kept haunting my every thought."

Beneath her hand, her heart slammed to a painful halt. "I find that difficult to believe."

A shockingly bleak expression tightened his profile. "No more than me. I kept hoping one morning I would awake and you would be gone. At last, I had to face the truth."

"What truth?"

"That I love you."

She took a shaken step backward, her eyes wide with disbelief.

"Oh . . ."

"I assure you it was not easy to accept."

"You cannot love me," she protested.

"But I do." Abruptly, he turned to stab her with a searing gaze. "I have loved you for years, but I allowed myself to be blinded by fear of duty and responsibility. Then I came back to Kent, and I was consumed by jealousy at the thought you cared more for Peter."

For so long she had battled to convince herself that Barth felt nothing for her. Now she regarded him with a wary suspicion.

"So you wanted revenge?"

"Yes. I just thought if I could rid myself of Mr. Effinton, you would once again love me."

"And now?"

A grimace twisted the handsome features. "Now I realize that I have always put my happiness before your own."

"Yes, you did," she rasped.

"No longer." He stepped closer. Close enough for her to smell the fresh scent of his skin. That frighteningly familiar sensation tightened the pit of her stomach. "My man of business will write to Peter and give him the information that he has suddenly acquired an inheritance from a distant cousin; he need never know that it came from me. He will be free to return to Kent and offer you marriage."

She searched his countenance, unable to accept his words. "And what of you?"

"Do not fear. I shall return to London and remain out of your life." His hand reached out to lightly stroke her cheek. "I only ask one thing."

Isa gave a violent shiver. "What?"

"That you be happy."

She gave a choked sob, the ice in her heart beginning to thaw. Was it possible? Would he indeed go so far as to sponsor Peter so that she could wed the man she claimed to prefer?

Could he indeed love her?

She raised a hand to her trembling lips. "Oh, Barth . . ."

He frowned, his hands moving to clasp her shoulders. "For God's sake, Isa, I did not come here to make you cry."

"I do not want to marry Peter," she shakily confessed, meeting the darkened hazel eyes. "It is you I love. Whom I have always loved, even when I did not wish to."

"Isa," he breathed, his hands tightening on her shoulders. For a moment, their gazes locked, as if each searching for assurance that their love had returned; then Barth abruptly pulled her into his arms. "My dearest Isa, tell me you will be my wife."

With her head pressed to his chest, Isa listened to the racing beat of his heart.

His wife.

For so long she had battled to avoid such a fate. Now a smile of deep pleasure curved her lips.

"Yes."

"Thank God." His lips pressed to her forehead. "I did not know how I would live without you."

She tilted back her head, shocked by the lingering pain that smoldered in the depths of his eyes.

"Were you really going to allow me to wed Peter?"

His gaze slowly lowered to the brilliant smile that shimmered through her tears.

"To see this smile, Isa, I would travel to the gates of hell. But . . ." His voice dropped to a husky pitch as he slowly lowered his head. "I would rather find heaven in your arms."

Definitely heaven, Isa dreamily conceded as his mouth found her lips in a kiss that made her heart trip in a most provocative manner. Tentatively, her own arms raised to encircle his neck, and she heard him give a satisfied moan deep in his throat.

With much reluctance, he at last pulled back to study the sheer happiness glowing upon her tiny face.

"It was just as the Gypsy promised," he softly quoted.

A love that is true
A heart that is steady
A wounded soul healed
A spirit made ready.
Three women will come
As the seasons will turn
And bring true love to each
Before the summer again burns. . . .

Isa offered him a shy smile. "So her blessing did work, after all."

He gave a satisfied smile. "Yes, indeed, and I have just forfeited a thousand pounds."

She gave a startled blink. "What?"

"Nothing of importance." A fierce heat flamed in the hazel eyes, making her knees oddly weak. "I was just about to find heaven. . . ."

ABOUT THE AUTHOR

Debbie Raleigh lives with her family in Missouri. Her next regency romance, *A Bride for Lord Brasleigh,* which will conclude her A Rose for Three Rakes trilogy, will be published in May 2001. Debbie loves to hear from readers, and you may write to her c/o Zebra Books. Please include a self-addressed stamped envelope if you wish a response.

BOOK YOUR PLACE ON OUR WEBSITE AND MAKE THE READING CONNECTION!

We've created a customized website just for our very special readers, where you can get the inside scoop on everything that's going on with Zebra, Pinnacle and Kensington books.

When you come online, you'll have the exciting opportunity to:

- View covers of upcoming books

- Read sample chapters

- Learn about our future publishing schedule (listed by publication month *and author*)

- Find out when your favorite authors will be visiting a city near you

- Search for and order backlist books from our online catalog

- Check out author bios and background information

- Send e-mail to your favorite authors

- Meet the Kensington staff online

- Join us in weekly chats with authors, readers and other guests

- Get writing guidelines

- AND MUCH MORE!

**Visit our website at
http://www.zebrabooks.com**